Other books by E. R. Wytrykus:

Novels: *The King of Coins*
The Money Run
A Stone To Roll
The Girls of His Dreams

Short Stories:
By The Short Hairs

Travelogue:
Travels With Gene & Gaye
(with Gaye Wytrykus)

All books published by and available from:
Wheat Field Publications
109 Kiwi Court
Lincoln, Ca. 95648
Wheatfieldpub@aol.com

The 9th Inning

a novella

and short stories:

The Prey
The Blue Blouse
The Kids

"The 9th Inning"

Copyright © 2010 E.R. Wytrykus
Published by Wheat Field Publications
109 Kiwi Court
Lincoln, Ca. 95648

ISBN: 978-0-9742216-8-7

Contents:

"The 9ᵗʰ Inning"

THE PITCHER

JACK SEVAN turned away from home plate and walked to the back of the pitcher's mound, rubbing the ball in his hands, warming it and feeling the seams in his fingers. It's funny how every baseball is the same, but each one has its own special feeling. At least that's how it is here, on the mound, even if they all look and feel the same when a dozen or so balls spill out of the ball bag.

The pitcher looked at the scoreboard, not that he needed a reminder of the situation. Jack Sevan seldom looked at the scoreboard during a game; there was no need to unless he was curious about the time and temperature. The status of the game he always knew. He knew his team, the Jets, led the game by a score of 2-0. He knew there was one out, and he knew he'd given up four hits today, one to the previous batter, Ben Train, who now stood at first base jawing with the first baseman. He knew he'd only walked one, that being the batter before Train, old grandpa Joe Havey. Harlem Joe stood on second base, arms folded and staring at his coaches, to see if they had any signs he needed to know about. Sevan glanced over at the third base coach, and as usual, like all coaches, he was gesturing with his arms and his hands, touching his nose or scratching his chin. None of his movements meant anything, Jack was sure, not at this stage of the game and with this situation and with this batter coming up. Havey was ancient, like most of everybody out here today, Jack realized, but he's the smartest base runner in the league, so no pinch runner for the old guy. Yeah, near everybody on both teams has seen their peak years. All the best young players are in the National or American Leagues, more's the shame.

Jack looked into the Jets' dugout to catch the eyes of his manager, Frank Jensen, who must be thinking about that base on balls Jack had surrendered, and then the sharply hit single by Train. Frank and Jack had been on the Jets together for more years than Jack wanted to think about. Frank had been the Jets' entrenched first baseman when Jack was signed by the Jets, and had rarely missed a game until he took over as manager. The two had had many a conversation on the mound in similar situations, more when Frank was playing first. You ever notice the first baseman or the third baseman never come over to talk to you unless they think you're in trouble?

Sevan caught Jensen's eyes and it was all the manager needed. In all his years, except for maybe the first couple when the pitcher was still raw and was more easily unsettled by a streak of wildness, or a rare stretch where no matter what pitch he offered up it was pounded back at twice the speed he'd thrown it, Sevan knew better than the manager and better than the catcher whether he was finished for the day or not. Besides, who else you gonna get to pitch against Dakota Keough with the tying runs on base, one out in the ninth, in the game that decides which of these two teams advances to the Championship Series? Well, okay, Johnny Zanto, the closer who had saved many a ball game for many a pitcher, including Sevan, and who now was tossing the ball softly in the bullpen. Jack laughed at the thought, knowing Johnny was making it look like he was just playing catch to keep from being bored, not like he might be getting ready to come in and put out this little brushfire Sevan had allowed to ignite.

Most any other time in a similar situation Sevan would stall a bit and give Zanto time to warm up, and the starting pitcher wouldn't be upset at all to come out of the game if he realized he'd thrown his last good pitch. When the stuff isn't good anymore or the arm is tired, you've got to accept it. Today though, with the game and the Division pennant on the line, Jack Sevan had felt the adrenalin flowing, felt extra strength in his left arm, the arm that had won its 300th game this season in a career that was now drawing to an end.

This was definitely no regular game. This was possibly Sevan's last game, that is, if he blew it. And he had no intention of blowing it, because if he did, old Johnny there in the bullpen would be mightily pissed that he'd finished the last game of his career tossing softballs in the bullpen.

It'd been quite a career; maybe not *the* Major Leagues, but the Continental League had held its own in exhibition games versus the 'Big Leaguers.' But economics had taken its toll, and the Continental was being absorbed, four franchises, including the Jets, joining the American and National Leagues next season. The top players would be signed after a draft, but the best of the old-timers, yeah, I'm one of them, Jack thought, maybe we'll be offered a minimum contract. Or maybe they'll give us free passes and say, "don't call us, we'll call you." Time marches on. Too old, they're saying. Yeah, well, maybe I'll just suck up my ego, sign for whatever, and go out and blew those big egos away.

"What the hell you doin', Jack?"

The voice of his catcher startled Sevan. He hadn't heard him come out to the mound.

"Oh, I was wondering if I should enter the draft or not. What're you gonna do?"

"God, man, not now. We got the winning run coming to bat! Get your mind straight!"

Sevan laughed. "You're so serious, Stevie! Rest easy; now, we gonna start Dak the usual way?"

"Sure. He'll be looking for it, but you put it where I ask and we'll get him. Now let's go. I'll flash some signs just to give Havey something to look at, but you know what to give me."

Jack turned his head to look at Joe Havey, standing with both feet planted on the bag, arms folded, the wrinkles under his big eyes visible from the mound. Jack grinned and Joe grinned back. They'd enjoy a steak together after game, loser buys, as usual.

"Ok, get your big butt back where it belongs and let's go," Jack said sharply.

Dakota Keough was the cleanup batter for the Cowboys, had been for many seasons. Sevan and Keough had faced each other countless times over the years, and of course the pitcher does come out ahead most of the time. But a batter can whiff three times in the course of the game, then blast a three-one fastball in his fourth at bat, and it doesn't matter any more that the pitcher struck him out three times previously. And Keough was the kind of batter who could hit any pitcher, you just never knew when. He was sort of a sleepy looking guy. Some of the players said Dak didn't get interested in the game until the seventh inning. Maybe so, maybe that's why the lore was that he was one of the best clutch hitters the league had ever seen. The statistics almost backed up the legend. Today had been one of those quiet games for him: three times up, three times down.

Steve Drake went into his crouch behind home plate. He flashed his fingers and Sevan pretended to pay attention, even so far as to shake his head twice. Joe Havey took a dainty lead off second base and glared at Drake's flying fingers. He watched, out of habit, but he knew that in this instance they meant nothing. If Havey was sure he picked up a hint of what was coming other than what Keough expected, he'd signal his teammate.

Keough had his strengths and weaknesses, like all batters. If pitchers could always put the ball in the exact spot they wanted, and get the exact break on their pitches that they wanted, each and every time, nobody'd ever get a hit. Baseball would be a complete bore because nobody could score a run. But pitchers can't always get the ball to do what they want. And when they slip up, that's when the batter needs to be on it. He may only get one pitch in a sequence that he can hit well, if he's lucky. Or one good one all damn game, for that matter.

So with Keough, as most batters, the pitchers knew how they wanted to pitch him, it was just a question of putting the ball in the spot the catcher asked for it. With Keough, Sevan usually started him out with a low inside pitch, to move him off the plate a little. Lots of pitchers did that to Keough. He knew it, and every so often the pitch didn't move inside enough, or low enough, and if he was ready, if he'd wiped the sleep out of his eyes, Dakota could send the ball to the moon. That, or a line drive foul that might behead the third baseman or threaten half the fans seated along the left field line.

When Sevan was on his game, as he was today, Drake wouldn't even need to move his glove. He could catch Sevan's pitches with his eyes closed. The first three times up for the Cowboy's cleanup

12

hitter had been frustratingly similar. First pitch, at his feet, kick up some dust, ball one. Dakota would remind himself to get back in his stance exactly where he'd been for the first pitch; don't edge away from the plate, because the next pitch will be outside.

Drake might as well have told Keough where each pitch was coming, the plan was so set. Pitch number two, a fastball, thumped into Drake's glove cutting the far edge of the plate. Not more than a seam flew across the black of the plate. The batter was tempted but Sevan was so quick early today that the ball was in Drake's glove before Keough could make up his mind. Strike one.

Jack was a notoriously fast worker and the umpires liked that. Too often for his own good a batter would ask for time when Sevan was already in his windup. If the umpire ignored the batter's request, Sevan would get an easy strike on a disoriented hitter. So Keough wanted to set the tone early, and asked for time-out even before Drake had returned the ball.

Keough was strong enough so that if he timed one of those pitches on the edge of the plate just right, he'd knocked it into the right centerfield upper deck. He'd even done that a time or two when Sevan was humming along. He set himself now and was sure the next pitch would be similar to the last one. It was, except that Drake had now set the target about three inches outside the strike zone. The eager Keough swung and missed the ball by so much he had to smile. Strike two.

The fourth pitch had again been inside and low and Keough figured he had as good a chance to hit it as he did waiting for another pitch, and he dribbled an easy roller to the third baseman, who threw Keough out with time to spare. Sevan was slightly disappointed he hadn't gotten a strike out, but the next two times up he fanned Keough with a similar sequence of pitches, fooling him totally on the third at bat by changing up his speed on strike three.

But Dak is smart, despite his seemingly lackadaisical attitude. Jack knew him, not real well, but had had enough conversations about subjects in or out of the baseball world to know the Cowboys' slugger was smarter than he looked.

When was that game, four, five years ago, a ditto situation. Us and the Cowboys neck and neck, last week of the season. I'd gotten him out three times easily, just like today. Tie ball game, bottom of the tenth, he powdered my best pitch. I didn't even turn to watch it, just walked off the mound, game over, they're in first. Yeah, they beat us that season, went on to beat the Texans for the Cowboys' only league title in the last decade. It was the only time in the last ten seasons that either the Jets or their archrivals the Texans hadn't won the championship.

The Texans had faded this season. Their great hitter, Mike Williams, had been hurt and missed most of the season. Their star pitcher, Frank Ford, the only pitcher in the league who could match up consistently with Sevan, had come down with a sore arm. He and Jack had only faced each other once this season, and both aces, maybe sensing that it was near the end of the line for them, had performed poorly. Neither had been involved in the decision and Jack couldn't even remember who won the game. He only remembered looking into the Texans' dugout when Frank had forlornly shuffled in having been relieved, and giving Frank a nod, a final salute to a great competitor. Frank had nodded back and then looked away, not wanting to share his disappointment with any one at that moment. No one else could understand how Frank felt at the time, except maybe another pitcher who'd been through the same traumas and elations, the same disappointment of not performing well in front of a big crowd, of letting your team down. But, oh, the joy of winning the big game cannot be fully appreciated except by someone who's been there.

Jack Sevan had been fortunate: never a sore arm and with several more victories in the second half of the season he had stretched his lead over Ford, and was now assured to go down in Continental League history as its winningest pitcher. Jack shared no such rivalry with any other pitcher in the league; there were some great ones, but none of the caliber of Sevan and Ford. So now Jack wished it was the Texans he was facing one last time, like in the best seasons when the two teams fought it out, often to the last game, and maybe again in the Championship Series. But life doesn't always work out the way you want it to. If it did, maybe Elaine would be sitting in the box seats, rooting for him.

On the other hand, Jack thought, maybe his first wife would be there and the second would never have existed. Two up, two down; he didn't think he'd give marriage a chance for strike three. Amazingly he found himself winding up, ready to pitch to Keough, with the thoughts of his wives overwhelming his attention to the game. Which is probably why his first pitch came in high and right over the center of the plate.

Keough was so surprised that he was late in his swing and was only able to hit a long foul ball that sliced into the stands. The catcher, Steve Drake, was shocked that Jack had missed his target by so much and trotted out to the mound.

"You okay? Are we on the same page?"

Jack stared at Drake, almost said something he'd regret. He and Drake had pitched and caught too many games together to argue now. Oh, sure, they'd had their disagreements about how to pitch certain batters, but in this case Steve was right and Jack was wrong. He hadn't been paying attention to his job.

"Yeah, yeah, sorry. I'm fine. The usual script, Stevie."

"You know, Johnny's almost warm, if you want him."

Jack's glare was his answer. Drake quickly retreated to his position behind the plate.

"You guys trying to throw me off, Steve?" asked Dakota Keough, a smile in his voice and on his face. He stepped back and gripped his bat, looking at it as if it could tell him where the hits were.

"We'll talk later Dak, let's go," Drake replied.

On the mound Sevan forced himself back into the game. Why thoughts of his wives, two beautiful women that he never had enough time for once they were married, came to him at this moment, he didn't understand. Unless it was because he knew this moment was special, win or lose, and he wished he'd have someone special to share it with after the game ended. Special that is, other than the guys. Oh, it'll be a great celebration if we win, and later we'll go out, and some wives will be there, and it'll be fun. And celebrating with the guys is fine, to a point. I just never seemed to find the time for her, either of them; dammit.

Jack closed his eyes and cleared his mind. He looked at Drake's glove and he looked at Keough's eyes, swore he saw a twinkle. Jack rarely looked at a batter while pitching to him. He knew too many of them on a personal basis and when he was working, the batter was the enemy. Jack knew who it was, knew his name, but whether it was a friend like Mike Williams of the Texans, or someone he had never gotten close to, like Keough, Jack had to work as if the batter wanted to steal Jack's job, and no mercy could be given. Later, after the game, maybe they'd chat about what had gone down, though it was a foolish person who gave away any secrets. Hell, what secrets, Keough knows what's coming, he just has to be ready and hope I make another mistake.

Jack's second pitch missed the right edge of the plate by a fraction of an inch. He thought he'd get the call and didn't grasp that the umpire, Jughead Bailey, had not indicated a strike, until he saw Drake stand up and give Bailey a dirty look. One and one. Doesn't changes anything, Sevan realized. Normally, he'd want to come a bit outside and try to get Keough to chase one. But if we didn't get that last call, we're not going to get him to bite on a pitch three inches outside, Jack thought. I usually go to two and one on him, anyway, so it's workable.

Jack again stepped off the mound and rubbed the ball. Havey stood a few feet off the bag and winked at Jack when he caught the pitcher looking his way. Good old Harlem Joe, what a player he has been. Football, baseball, I think he even played some semi-pro basketball. He never ran out of a sports season. How the hell did he keep his marriage together all these years? Jack had the irrational urge to walk over to second base and ask Havey what was the secret of making his marriage last. Geez, Jensen would yank me in a flash. Jack actually laughed and Havey thought it was because of his wink. Jack turned back to the mound and gave a nearly imperceptible kick sideways with his left foot, just an inch.

Steve Drake saw Sevan's sign, as did the Jets' second baseman, Bill Brick. Jensen, the Jets' manager saw it and approved. Lots of people probably saw it but didn't know the significance. Havey might guess, Sevan thought, if he noticed it, or one of his coaches might warn him. If they did, Sevan would hear them call out to Havey and then Jack could cancel the attempted pick off. It wasn't a play he tried often and it was risky in this situation. If Bill missed the sign, or I throw the ball away, the Texans could soon have men on second and third.

Sevan stared intently at Drake's fingers. He saw the sign he wanted, the one that said Bill Brick had noted Sevan's little kick and was ready. If Havey didn't take much of a lead Drake would give another signal and call off the play. But it looked to be a go.

Keough stood in, crowding the plate, daring Sevan to give him one high and tight. Havey took his lead, stretching it a bit more than he had on the first two pitches, because he had felt sure Keough would not even swing at the first two. But this pitch could be put into play.

Sevan readied, turned to look at Havey, pretending unconcern about the length of his lead, looked again at Drake, then pivoted and fired to second base. Bill Brick moved like a ballerina, but Havey had sensed something and began to move back towards the base a split second before Sevan threw. He dived at the bag and touched it just as Brick slapped the tag on him.

"Safe!" the umpire cried.

"Oh, man, we had him," grumbled Brick.

Havey stood up, dusted himself off, and glanced into the dugout, afraid he'd be removed for a pinch runner. Sevan watched him and wondered the same thing, but knew that would be embarrassing

18

for the old star. The Cowboys' coaches should be embarrassed, too, for missing the play, so leave him alone. Smart move would be to put a faster runner in, but old Joe was a savvy pro. Brick grinned at Havey and threw the ball back to Sevan. "We had ya, Joe."

"Tie goes to the runner," Havey said, as he took a short lead off the base, trying to show he wasn't cowed by the near pickoff.

Sevan readied for his next pitch quickly, hoping to startle Keough. He fired it at Drake's glove, three inches outside, and hit the spot perfectly. Keough stood still.

"Ball two," Umpire Bailey said, to no one's surprise.

It's amazing, Sevan reflected, how many thoughts can pass through one's mind in the span of a few seconds. It's also amazing that in my entire career I've not thought about anything while pitching except the job at hand. Now, maybe my last game, maybe my last pitch, and I can't get Ellen out of my mind. Or is it Elaine I'm thinking of? Sometimes the two faces merge together, sometimes I can't remember which one came first, or who's Bobby's Mom and who is Lily Ann's Mom.

He rubbed the ball, glanced at the runners, and got it straight: Ellen was first, and after three years we had Bobby, then two years later it all fell apart. What the hell, she actually expected me to give up pitching, the only thing I'm any good at. Damn, she knew what I did when we got married! Met her at a ball game, Jensen's wife's friend. I already had a career, what the hell was she thinking? Before we were married she never suggested she wanted me to quit.

Yeah, hell, I missed not having time with her and Bobby, who wouldn't? All the guys said the same thing, but it's the job. And then Elaine, same thing. She said she thought I'd quit after we had Lily

Ann; where the hell'd she get such a crazy idea? Okay, let's go, two and one, get ready Dak.

Sevan checked the signs to make sure nothing was on, just in case Brick or Drake wanted to try the pickoff again. He looked over his left shoulder at Havey standing near second base. The runner's lead was shorter than it had been. Heh, the pickoff try did do something; could make the difference on a play at the plate.

Well, balls and strikes, there ain't gonna be any play at the plate if I can help it. Sevan stretched and aimed at Keough's knees. The ball sped towards the batter, then began to move in toward the plate, just as Sevan had planned. It didn't appear to be moving as much as he expected. Shit, this might hang there, Sevan thought, already planning to move behind the plate to cover a possible play if Keough powdered the pitch to a gap in the outfield.

As in slow motion Sevan watched his pitch zipping towards Keough, then sliding away, millimeter by millimeter. He saw Keough's eyes widen as the batter gauged where the ball would be when he could get the fat part of his bat on it. Then, almost a miracle, but then, that's what I expected, this is what I do, the ball broke away sharply and the thud of it hitting Steve Drake's mitt and the swish of Keough's bat hitting nothing but air brought cheers from the crowd. Few of the masses noticed the quick toss Drake made to first base to keep the runner honest.

The first baseman, Don Sandusky began to throw the ball back to Sevan, then stuck it in his glove and reached back quickly to tag the runner, who was standing solidly on first.

"Don't swat me, Don, I'm not going anywhere--yet," said Ben Train.

Sandusky smirked and tossed the ball back to Sevan.

What was it Elaine wanted me to do? Oh, yeah, coach at the local college. Great, give up being the ace of the league, give up the money, give up the cheers of the crowd, the adoration of the fans and teammates, to coach a bunch of kids. Later, yeah, when I'm retired, that'd be fine. Next thing you know she'd had me coaching frickin' soccer!

Okay, two and two, where do you want it, Stevie, Sevan asked silently, eager to get to the next pitch. Do we go for the K or try to get him to beat it into the ground for a DP? Dak doesn't move so well these days; hell, do any of us? If I can get him to ground it we can go home.

Yet his mind wandered, to last season, to that fantastic season-ending series against the Texans, when the two teams went down to the last game tied for the best record in the league, battling for home field advantage. Now, after 119 games it all came down to this one game, and who would go to the Continental League Championship Series. Those were the greatest days, when the Jets and Texans often battled all season down to the last series between the two, and frequently to the last game of the Championship Series itself. Damn, I wish it was Mike I was facing here, just for the challenge.

What season was it that I hit him with the bases loaded, bringing in the tying run? Man, was Mike pissed! He thought I did it on purpose even if it did tie the game. Hell, I'm not sure I didn't to it on purpose, better than have him win the game with a base hit. But no, I always liked to go straight at the top dogs. I never dallied with Mike Williams, no, I'd go after him fastball after fastball, you or me, can you time this one or not. That last time I got him with three high hard ones in a row, the winning run on base, two out in the ninth. Jensen had a fit, giving him pitches up there where Williams loved 'em.

But this time it was Keough and he was challenge enough. These kinds of challenges I can handle, but I couldn't handle the ones Ellen and Elaine threw at me. Funny thing is, what got me was when she said I loved to be on the road because of all the skirts chasing the ball players. If there was anything I didn't do, it was play around. Who was it, Ellen or Elaine that accused me? No matter, it wasn't true.

It's not like I really enjoyed being on the road once we were married, but I couldn't help it. I love the crowds, Jack admitted, stepping back and looking out at the throng, thinking this must have been what it was like for the greatest gladiator to enter the Coliseum. Not much of a crowd compared to the old days. Ah, it's a shame Williams got hurt; we didn't get to go at each other much at all this season. I wonder if he's here in the park, rooting for me or against me?

Just as the catcher rose up from his crouch, getting irritated with the dawdling of his battery mate, Sevan was ready. Drake hunched down and gave Jack the signal—outside and low, nowhere near where Keough can reach it, and if he does, the best he'll do is bounce and easy hopper to Brick at second base.

A glance at the runners to keep them honest and Sevan gripped and threw his fifth pitch of the sequence. The ball tailed away from the batter, as Drake had wanted and for a nanosecond it looked like Keough would bite. But he held up and the pitch was clearly outside and low, ball three. One pitch away from loading the bases, but neither Drake nor Sevan feared that. If there was one thing Sevan had not lost once he'd found it, it was his control.

Man, I was a wild one, like Sandy Koufax when I first came up. Wes De Angelo was the pitching coach who took me under his guidance, Sevan recalled. Tightened up one little move with my footwork and it was like the clouds cleared on a stormy day and the angels sang Hosanna. You've got it, my boy! From then on Sevan rarely walked anyone unintentionally, and with this control came control of his youthful temper, which had reared its ugly head when he couldn't find the plate. No walks, no bad temper.

But I did get mad when Ellen accused me of running around. Or was it Elaine? No, she was the one who wouldn't even bring Lily Ann to the games during the summer; said she needed to play with her friends. Well, duh, bring all her friends, I can get tickets!

Okay, okay, pay attention to business, Sevan, this is getting serious now. Think baseball, not ex-wives. Three and two, so it's show time. Inside, but not too much, high, but not too high, and fast. He knows it's coming, Drake knows it's coming, even Jughead Bailey behind the plate knows it's coming. The fans know it's coming and with their anticipation the buzz from the crowd begins to swell. The fans stood, cheering for strike three, many forgetting that there would still be only two outs even if Keough did fan. Sevan could see Keough and Drake saying something. What the hell do they have to talk about?

The pitch was right where Drake and Sevan wanted it, and right where Keough expected it to be. He was ready and in his hey-day he might have connected cleanly. But like most of the players in the league he was older and slower. The reflexes weren't what they used to be. He did knick the ball, just hard enough that the catcher couldn't hold on to it. The ball trickled away in the dirt and Bailey handed a bright, new one to Drake. The crowd oohed and sat down. Naturally, a foul ball on three and two, let's do it again.

I remember the time Williams fouled off a dozen pitches, maybe more. Most of them long bombs, but all foul. We were almost running out of baseballs. It was an early season game, not much on the line, and Mike started to laugh. He stood there at home plate and couldn't stop himself. Next thing you know I'm laughing, then Drake takes off his mask and tries to spit out the dust, but he starts laughing and the spit dribbles down his chin. So Mike starts laughing all the more. The umpire finally quieted us down but when I started to pitch I just broke up. There was a runner on first, so I got called for a balk. Finally I managed to throw something, but I was still laughing and the ball sort of flopped out of my hand. Williams saw this pumpkin coming at him with nothing on it, took a roundhouse swing, even as he began to laugh, and popped up the sucker. He lost his balance and fell down, laughing so hard he couldn't get up to run. God, those were some days!

Jack covered his face with his glove for a few seconds while he got rid of the grin. But he'd taken so long that by now Keough had asked for time, got it, and stepped out of the batter's box. Some fans booed, the hometown crowds blaming Keough for stalling. Jack almost laughed again.

Okay, Sevan, get with it. He forced to empty his mind of any other thoughts, of ex-wives, of kids, of great games he'd won, of frustrating loses, of arguments with umpires and wives, of celebrations and last minute defeats, of teammates and rivals, of friendships that had outlasted balls and strikes, runs and outs, of divorce papers and lawyers.

24

Sevan stared at Keough; his mind clear again, he wanted to work quickly. Then, when everyone was ready, and just because he knew doing it would agitate Keough, Sevan tossed the ball to first, an obviously lazy pickoff attempt.

Keough shook his head, stepped back and asked for time. He kicked at the dirt in the batter's box until he had moved it around and probably back to where it was before he started. Drake smiled behind his mask and nonchalantly touched the side of his mask. Sevan caught the sign, a change in the usual progression of pitches. He nodded his agreement, then stared at Keough. Sevan realized that out or not, Jensen might insist on bringing in Johnny to get the final out. So this may be my last pitch.

The buzz began again and twenty thousand and some odd number of people rose up yelling and whistling and clapping their hands. Joe Havey on second base edged away from safety, extending his lead a bit more than he had on the last couple of pitches. He glanced around to be sure neither the shortstop nor the second baseman was sneaking close to the bag. Ben Train on first took his lead, a moderate one; he knew he wasn't going anywhere unless Havey was able to advance. The third baseman inched away from third base a bit; they'd decided not to pitch him inside. Sevan waited patiently for Keough to get in the box, to get a good stance; he wanted to see his eyes. Sevan stretched and threw.

THE BATTER

DAKOTA KEOUGH dragged himself from the on deck circle to the batter's box. He kicked at the dirt as much out of habit as any other reason. He was surprised he was getting another chance to bat. The way Sevan's been throwing today I figured it'd be another three up, three down inning, ball game, season. But the old rascal must be tiring, giving a pass to Havey, then a single to Ben. Now me, lucky me.

Damn Sevan, I've never done well against him. Pisses me off, too, 'cause I always know what's coming. First pitch, at my ankles, every time; it's a game with him. Once, once I managed to golf one of those into the bleachers, shocked hell out of Sevan and me and everybody in the stadium. Gotta give the old fart credit, I guess, he seems to be toughest on the toughest. Handcuffed me three straight times today.

Dakota was sort of a sleepy looking guy. Some of the players said Dak didn't get interested in the game until the seventh inning. Maybe so, but he was ready now, as ready as he'd ever be. Like Sevan and most of the other players on the field, Dakota knew this was likely the last hurrah. He was pushing forty years old and with the end of the Continental League there was no place for him to go. Maybe a coaching job in Triple A.

On the mound Sevan seemed to be daydreaming. Maybe he was stalling, giving Zanto more time to warm up. Not likely I'll get to face Johnny Zanto, my old buddy from the sandlot days. Funny thing is, Zanto, the best reliever in the league, I hit pretty well. He made me promise to give him my secret when we're retired, but I don't have any damn secret. Just lucky against him. No, Jensen's not gonna let me have a hack at Johnny.

Well, shit, now Drake's going out to gab with Sevan. What the hell do they need to talk about?

"For Christ's sake, Jugs, let's go," Dakota said to the umpire.

"A second, Dak."

"They're stalling."

Archie 'Jughead' Bailey took off his mask and stepped over home plate, just as Steve Drake began to trot back to his position.

"You guys ready to play ball?" asked Bailey.

"Yessir. Jack's getting nostalgic out there."

Keough set the bat down on the ground, holding it between his legs, reached down for dirt and rubbed it in his hands. He was a stubborn old-timer—no batting gloves for him, dirt to dry off the hands and get a good grip. Bunch of pansies and their gloves.

He stepped in, took his stance, slightly crowding the plate, and looked out at Sevan. The pitch came and instantly Keough was shocked. The pitch looked perfect, for him, that is. Right in my zone, the batter thought. Had he been younger, maybe just a year younger, or had he been mentally more prepared for the possibility that the first pitch wouldn't be a wasted one, Keough might have stunned Sevan and Drake, and twenty thousand Jets fans. But he was just a bit late, too surprised to take advantage of Sevan's error. He swung with great gusto but hit the ball with the thin part of the bat, a long foul ball souvenir. Goddamn, he muttered.

He watched as the catcher, Steve Drake, hustled to the mound. It was a mistake, that's for sure. Drake needs to know what's going on.

"Fuck, Jugs, I shoulda killed that one."

"Shoulda, coulda, woulda," replied the umpire.

Keough grunted.

As Drake came back to his position, Keough said to him, "You guys trying to throw me off, Steve?"

"We'll talk later Dak, let's go," Drake replied.

Keough tapped the plate with his bat, getting his distance and stance in alignment. Expected it to be one and oh, but they've got a strike on me already, so I know this pitch ain't gonna be anywhere I can reach. Still, Sevan may be slipping a bit, getting tired.

Yeah, aren't we all getting tired. Seems the fun's gone out of it, I dunno. We knew this day would come, all of us. The league couldn't stay together anymore. Hell, the core fans are older than us, the young baseball fans watch the National and American Leagues on TV. Or worse, they play video baseball; fuck that.

The second pitch was also a surprise in that it wasn't as far outside as Keough expected. In fact, for an instant Keough feared Bailey would call a strike, but after the briefest of hesitations, he mumbled "Ball one". Shit, I might have poked that sucker to right center. Fucker is playing with my mind.

Now what's he doing, Keough wondered, as he noticed Sevan kicking dirt on the mound. Never mind, get ready, he may come back inside on me. Keough had the flash of an idea, that he would bunt the ball towards third. Ha, would that surprise 'em! Trouble is, I'd probably fall down trying to beat it out. Now what the…

Sevan whirled and fired the ball to second base, trying to pick off Joe Havey. "Oh, that was close!" Keough said.

"Hot damn, I thought we had him!" cried Drake.

Keough saw Havey and the second baseman, Bill Brick, saying something to each other, mild smiles on their faces. One thing about this league, is the players generally all liked one another. There never were that many of us, only eight teams, and if one of us was traded it was to a team where we already knew the other guys. There was never a lot of money in the league so even the superstars didn't get paid so much more than the others that it created tension. So what if it wasn't *the Majors*, as in the American and National Leagues. The last thought sat there, rolling gently in Keough's mind. Oh, but that would have been something, the Majors.

A noise, shouts from the stands, all those damn Jets' fans, jarred Keough and brought him back into the game. He looked out at the mound just as Sevan was getting set. He stood in, telling himself to wake up and be ready. Christ, the last thing I want is for people to say I was asleep at the plate in my last at bat!

The pitch was way outside, exactly where Drake had placed his mitt.

"Ball two," Umpire Bailey said, merely stating the fact.

Now Sevan, I never did know very well. Talked to him, sure, but I don't remember any substantial conversations we had other than about baseball. Batted against him hundreds of times, even went to dinner with him a few times after a game, always with a group though. They tell me he was a rather serious guy, fun to be around, yeah, but a pretty straight shooter on the road. No gambling, no screwing around. Read books and went to old movies. Married two beautiful gals and couldn't keep either, wonder why that was.

Keough stepped back and checked his coaches for signs. He couldn't imagine there'd be anything he needed to know, but those fools were always jumping around, picking their nose or scratching their balls. Most of the time the signs meant nothing. I don't think we're gonna run a double steal now, not with the tying run on second base. Okay, get your ass ready, Keough.

The ball left Sevan's hand, a white blur speeding towards Keough at ninety plus miles per hour. It looks good, hittable if I can get the fat part of the bat on it. There was no way Keough was actually thinking a viable thought at that moment. There wasn't time to think. The best hitters reacted; think before the pitch, think about it later maybe, but when the ball's flying at you and you need to stand still or make your move, there's no time to think about should I or shouldn't I.

Dakota Keough's eyes widened as he followed the movement of the spheroid. He swung, seeing the ball, or imagining he saw it, just inches from his bat as he did so. Then it was gone. It had moved, somewhere, gone from his sight. The thud of it hitting Steve Drake's mitt and the swish of Keough's bat hitting nothing but air brought cheers from the crowd.

"Fuckin' A," gasped Keough, who spat in the dirt and didn't notice that Drake had whipped the ball to first trying for a pickoff.

"Steerike!" yelled Bailey.

There comes a time when a batter knows he is overpowered. The pitcher is toying with him, setting him up for the kill, but when he wants to, not a pitch sooner. Goddammit, Sevan, not this time, thought Keough. Last chance for one of us, and I want it to be me. I won't let you beat me this time.

Keough had nothing to be ashamed of. Two home run titles, twice leading the league in runs batted in, a decent lifetime batting average, the all-star game nearly every season, and a couple of league championships. One more would be nice. Would have been more titles if it hadn't been for Lucky and Williams; those two were always edging me out. Ah, fuck it.

Keough could hear the crowd, primarily a Jets crowd, of course, but even here the crowds were nowhere near what they used to be. Without television revenue, with less and less people caring about that 'other' league, there was no way we could survive. Well, begorrah, it's been a good run.

Sevan was fiddling around out there again. I don't know if he's stalling for Zanto to warm up, not sure what to do, or just dragging this out because, like me, he doesn't want it to end. No, even the times I struck out with the bases loaded, and lord knows there have been plenty of those times; I wouldn't trade them for nothing. Nobody will ever take away the thrills, the excitement, the plain goddamn fun of it all. Yeah, we're just a bunch of kids playing ball. You ever hear anybody say we *work* ball? No, we *play* ball.

"We're gonna be here all day, Jugs. Sevan can't decide what he wants to do," Keough said.

"What, you got a hot date?"

Keough laughed and Drake, who had stood up and began to move out to the mound, got back into his crouch.

"Get ready, Dak, I don't want you to say you weren't ready."

"Bring it on, Stevie."

The pitch didn't tempt Keough. It was outside, much too low, nothing he needed to worry about. Full count, game time.

Sevan doesn't walk many, that's for sure, and I don't think he's going to now. He gets beat, he wants to go down fighting, and so do fuckin' I. This'll be close enough I have to swing, I'm sure, but not too good. I feel it, I'm there, and I am ready for you, Sevan.

He heard the crowd, yet he didn't, not really. It was just there in the background, a buzz, a horde of bees, a buzz that could have been for him or against him, it didn't matter. Someone yelled, "Strike the bum out!"

"Listen to that crowd," the catcher said.

"Oh, hell," said Keough, "that ain't nothin'. You ever been to Yankee Stadium?"

The pitch was about where Keough was expecting it, inside, not high enough for his liking, tough to do much with, but close enough to the strike zone that he had to bite. Like with the first pitch, it was one that in his younger days he could have handled. Of course, in Sevan's younger days it would have come in five or six miles per hour faster, and no one this side of 'The Natural' could have hit it.

He stayed alive, Keough did, getting enough of the ball to send it spinning in the dirt, sending the runners back to their bases, and quieting the buzz, momentarily. "Dammit!" Keough said.

Don't think, Dakota, the batter told himself. No, he didn't tell himself, the thought was just there, an instinct no different than ones that tell birds to fly south for the winter. Just get ready, get a grip, and pound it.

Dakota Keough, all-time Cowboy's home run hitter, sleepy-eyed or not, set himself into a comfortable stance, readying for the climax of this sequence. He'd done this many times, so it was automatic. Yet, this time it was not an at bat to be taken casually. It was one he would remember, no matter the outcome. If he struck out, he wanted to know he'd been ready, he'd been prepared. If I go down, I'll go down with my best hacks.

He should have known Sevan would do that. A toss to first, an easy lob, not a serious attempt to pick off the runner, but just something to throw off the batter's concentration. What the fuck, who's he think he's dealing with, some rookie, Keough thought. So now he'll wait for me.

Keough stepped back, muttering, picked up more dirt to rub on his hands, then held up one hand to the umpire for time, while he rearranged the dirt in the batter's box with his right foot. He took more time than was necessary but the ump didn't rush him. Finally he settled in.

Keough stuck his bat out, pointing it towards the pitcher, and saw Sevan look at the catcher, nod, and turn his gaze towards his enemy. Keough was positive that Sevan's nod was nothing more than consensus at the planned location of the pitch. When Keough looked towards the mound he caught Sevan staring directly at Keough's eyes. The Cowboy's slugger stared back, the two pair of eyes passing a private signal. Let me see your fastball, Jack, fire it in here. The pitcher stretched and threw.

THE MANAGER

FRANK JENSEN picked at his gray mustache and stared at his pitcher. Sevan was walking around the backside of the mound, looking at the scoreboard and for the most part avoiding looking at the manager. Jensen was patient. He knew he wasn't going to take Sevan out just yet, lest his ace indicated he was finished for the day. And Jensen knew from Sevan's body language that wasn't the case yet.

Every time this happens I have to remind myself I am the manager, and if I want to take him out, I can. But Keough is coming up and he hits Zanto better than he hits Sevan. Finally, Sevan turned towards the dugout to catch the eyes of Jensen. It was all that needed to be said.

Frank would stand in the dugout, one foot up on the edge, one hand covering his mouth, and not move for minutes at a time. Except for his eyes, which darted around the field, from player to player. He would send signals with his eyes, or by just a slight movement of his hand over his mouth or by rubbing his mustache. Rubbing it right to left might mean a pitch out; left to right could mean move a certain fielder closer to the line. The meaning changed from game to game.

Jensen had been involved in the game of baseball too long to get too excited about any particular situation. He knew what the players had to do, and all he could do was give them guidance. He'd been through devastating losses, but he'd also been involved in more championships, as player and manager, than anyone in the history of the Continental League.

The stories were legion, and a few were true. Jensen had started out as a pitcher, and wasn't bad, but his control was erratic. He

34

once walked five batters in a row before striking out the side. Another time he walked the first three batters in the ninth inning of a game his team was leading 1-0, and he had a no-hitter going. His manager took him out of the game, and the momentary delay by Jensen in relinquishing the ball cost him a fine and a demotion back to the minors. When he came back up he was a first baseman. But he and the Texans' manager never did see eye to eye. So in what is still considered the worst trade in the history of the league, the Texans traded Jensen to the Jets for a two highly-rated pitching prospects, whose names are long forgotten.

Jensen went on to become the most feared slugging first baseman and led the Jets to the league championship in his first season. A few years later, when players like Jack Sevan and outfielder Al Lucky joined the Jets, they became so powerful there were cries of "break up the Jets."

Jensen was tough and mean looking, but he was a pussycat. He played hurt, he played hard, he played in the 9th inning of a 10-0 game as if it was the first inning. He never came out of a game, setting consecutive game and innings records that could never be broken. Of course, with the league disbanding, it was one of several of his records that would now last forever, or at least as long as anyone was interested in keeping the league's records.

When his consecutive game streak did end it was late in a game the Jets had well in hand, and Jensen had to be forced off the field. Jensen had collapsed while running out a ball hit to right field, and he crawled the last few feet to first base. Turned out he had appendicitis and needed immediate surgery. Since the season had ended he had time to rest, but the Jets didn't start him the first three games of the

Championship Series against the Texans, which made Jensen very angry.

Down two games to nothing, and trailing the Texans 2-0 in the 9th inning, the Texans' ace Frank Ford mowing done the Jets like it was a backyard whiffle ball game, the Jets put two runners on with two outs. Their light-hitting shortstop was due up and Jensen walked over to manager John Olzsewski with his bat in his hand and looked at Big John O without saying a word. Olzsewski had been one of the first stars of the league and in the last few seasons, even as manager, remained a rostered player and a pinch-hitter supreme. He toyed with going to bat himself but the look on Jensen's face convinced him otherwise. He nodded and Jensen marched to the batter's box.

The way they tell the story now, Jensen had collapsed in batting practice, been taken away for an appendectomy, snuck out of the hospital, hailed a cab while still wearing his hospital garb with his big rear end sticking out the back, and arrived at the ball park just as the ninth inning started.

They say that when he came to bat there was blood on his side and that on the first two swings he missed and fell down. Like something out of a corny movie Jensen somehow managed, ala Kirk Gibson, to connect on the next pitch for the winning grand slam home run to win the seventh and deciding game.

The truth is almost as good. It wasn't a grand slam, it was a three run homer, and it did win the game. It was hit off the great Frank Ford, but it was only the third game, and the Texans went on to win the series in six when Ford started again and threw a two-hit shutout, striking out Jensen three times. But it still makes for a good story. In fact, Jensen said Ford fooled him. He expected a fastball, got a curve, but it hung and he had time to adjust. "I was damn lucky, that's all," Jensen said whenever the subject came up. But he didn't argue the point too much. No matter, such stories are fun; they become tall tales, and eventually they become legends.

Jensen silently stood still watching as his catcher went to the mound to confer with Sevan. Jack does seem to be taking his time, but that could be a ploy to aggravate Keough. It will also give Zanto more time to heat up. He turned to his pitching coach and flicked a finger. Jim Roberts reached for the bullpen phone. If the next batter gets on, Zanto is in, so pick up the pace, he told the bullpen coach.

Jensen reviewed the situation in his mind. He knew Havey on second base had lost a step or two, thank you, Father Time. If Keough gets a hit to the outfield the fielder is going to have to decide whether he can throw to the plate to try to nab Havey. Likely they'll play it safe, but if Harlem Joe takes a big lead, somewhere in this sequence Drake or Sevan might want to consider a pickoff.

If he were prone to cringing, Jensen would have when Sevan's pitch came into Keough's power zone. Lucky, he muttered quietly, when Keough only produced a long, loud foul ball.

"Oh, shit man, that was close!" someone in the dugout hollered.

For all his reputation of being mean and tough, Frank Jensen never used foul language, except maybe under his breath when no one could hear him. He didn't say much at all, actually. "Good game", he told Sevan after Jack had no-hit the Alouettes, high praise, indeed.

Jensen watched as Drake went to the mound again. They need to straighten something out. Jack is tiring, no doubt, but he'd fight me on the mound if I tried to take him out now. No, he has to do this, or at least give it his best shot. Our last shot, all of us; certainly for old-timers like me and Sevan, Phillips, Zanto… yeah, hell of a career we've had. He saw Sevan give Drake a dirty look and knew that the catcher had dared to question whether Jack still had enough gas. Drake should know better.

The manager shuffled his foot and moved his left hand a few inches. The right fielder, Al Lucky, edged a few feet to the right field foul line in response to the sign. Jensen ran his hand over his face as he brought it down, and Drake saw it. The catcher in turn scratched his knee and Sevan knew that Jensen wanted them to think about Havey's lead off second base.

Watching Sevan Jensen was reminded of himself. He had started out on the mound. But could never get consistent control. Sevan started the same way, as I recall. Wild, cocky, temperamental, and brimming with talent. All he needed was control. Once he got it, everything settled down for him. He'd been getting mad at himself and when the control came, he was happy as a lark. Never could figure out why he and Ellen hadn't lasted. They were a great couple. I guess Jack couldn't give her the attention he gave to baseball. Then the other one, Elaine, such a beautiful girl, but pushy, and Jack didn't like to be pushed. A shame for Jack; he has talents and success, acclaim and awards, couple of nice kids, but two failed marriages. Who can figure it?

Frank's own wife of thirty years had died fairly young, of cancer. If I hadn't had baseball then, a job that took so much of my time, I would have gone crazy, Frank admitted. Liz, bless her, loved baseball. I guess that was the difference for Jack and me. His wives didn't love baseball.

38

For a heartbeat Frank thought the Jets would get the call on the second pitch to Keough. It was close enough to go either way. But not close enough to make a stink of it. Keough did good to hold up on it.

He glanced at Havey on second base, at his second baseman, Bill Brick, and back to Sevan. He saw Jack kick some dirt and he refrained from moving his eyes towards second base, lest he give a hint.

If Jensen ever wanted to curse, he would have on the pickoff play.

"Safe!" the umpire cried.

"Oh, man, we had him," grumbled Brick.

"C'mon Lester!" someone in the dugout yelled at the second base umpire.

The pitching coach, Jim Roberts moved next to Jensen. "Johnny'll be ready in a minute."

"If Keough gets on, I may need you to help me drag Jack off the mound."

Roberts snickered. "I don't think so. Jack wants to finish it, but if hasn't got enough to get Keough, he'll know he needs to come out. Drake will convince him."

Jensen nodded, said nothing as the next pitch, clearly a ball, made the count two and one. Just where they expected to be at this point. Just don't get careless now, Jack.

"I shouldn't say this, don't want to jinks us, but Jack's always handled Keough pretty well. He'll get him."

Jensen nodded and added an uncomfortable grunt.

Sevan's pitch flew towards the plate and Jensen and Roberts watched as Keough took a big swing and missed, the pitch cutting away from him at the last blink. Jensen watched the catcher's quick throw to first base, then glanced at Sevan. From the look in his pitcher's eyes Jensen suspected the ball had not moved quite the way Sevan had expected, just good enough.

"Oh, that always scares me!" said Roberts.

Jensen looked at him, not understanding.

"Throwing to first in this situation; ball goes into right field both runners score."

Jensen spat. "How often you see Stevie throw one into right field?"

Roberts shrugged.

"He is tiring," the manager said. Roberts agreed but didn't say anything. The phone buzzed. "That means Johnny's ready," Roberts said, unnecessarily.

"Don't screw around, now, Jack," Jensen said, so softly even the coach, Roberts, next to him, couldn't hear. Sometimes Jack likes to go at the batter like a bullfighter against El Toro. You and me, as if he had no back up, no fielders, no catcher to suggest a target. His only weakness was that once in awhile Jack forgets the situation and gets more wrapped up in trying to outmuscle the hitter, when all you have to do is outsmart him.

Sevan's next pitch was about like the third one. As it dived in Jensen hoped Keough would go for it; double play ball, tailor-made. But Keough, not always the most patient of hitters, didn't bite. Full count.

"Here we go," said Roberts.

"Let's go Jackie boy!" was one of the screams Jensen could hear from behind the dugout. Most of the fans where Jets fans, of course, home park and all. Some of them Jensen knew by first name, they'd been to so many games, so many years, rain or shine, good team or bad. What are they gonna do with all their time, he wondered.

Foul ball, said Jensen, to himself, even before the pitch arrived in Keough's vicinity. The veteran manager could see the ball was going to be high and tight, almost what Keough liked, but a pitch Jensen didn't think he could handle cleanly, and he didn't, the ball spinning off his bat into the ground, kicking up a mini dust devil.

"Three years ago Dakota would have killed that pitch," Roberts said.

"Three years ago it would have past him before he started his swing," countered Jensen.

"Hmm, yeah."

Jensen slapped his hands together, spat, and whispered, "Let's go, Jack, all I want is one more strike out of you."

The pitching coach smiled at Jensen in surprise. That was almost a speech, coming from the taciturn manager.

Neither one said a word as Sevan lobbed the ball to the first baseman, not expecting to surprise the runner, but just to irritate the batter. Nothing new.

Jensen's eyes moved quickly around the field, at every one of his players. The third baseman, Cal Richards, inched toward third base a step; he expected that the next pitch would be inside; if Keough did connect, it likely would come sharply towards the foul line. An instant later, just before the pitch, Richards shuffled back to his left, adjusting his position one more time, setting up closer to the shortstop, who also moved a step to his left.

Lucky, in right field, had moved more towards center before the prior pitch without Jensen having to signal him. He watched Keough as he kicked dirt in the batter's box until he had moved it around and probably back to where it was before he started. He watched his catcher, Steve Drake, smile at the batter's antics, he saw Sevan stare at the catcher and nod. He watched the runners take their lead. He turned his full attention to his pitcher, and stood up straight as Sevan threw.

THE RUNNERS

BEN TRAIN and JOE HAVEY took their leads, Train off first base, Joe off of second. Harlem Joe, Havey was called, after his place of birth in New York City, the son of a Creole jazz musician and a white, Irish cleaning woman.

Joe used the cliché, 'the school of hard knocks', to describe his childhood in the streets of Harlem, often fighting his way to and from school, that is, on those days when he went to school. It took him an extra year to finish high school, and if it hadn't been for sports and the insistence of his mother, he never would have bothered.

In high school he starred on the track team and the basketball team, and would have been on the football and baseball teams, too, except the school didn't offer those sports. The school district didn't have the funds for sports that required expensive uniforms and equipment. Joe also learned to play the saxophone from his father, and the money he earned from gigs, which his mother arranged to be paid to her, not Joe, was enough to get him into a small college in New Jersey.

Joe's father wasn't interested in raising kids, he only cared about his music, so he didn't interfere with his wife's plans for Joe. He wouldn't have minded if Joe had just learned to play jazz and forgot sports and schooling, but his wife was adamant that Joe needed to go to college. So off he went, hitchhiking his way with all his belongings in a gym bag, and the sax over his shoulder.

His grades were awful, but he set school records in several track events and led the basketball team to an undefeated season, albeit in a small league barely known outside a twelve-block radius of Southwest New Jersey Technical College.

Why Warner Coleman went to a basketball game between the small New Jersey College and a high school from Newark is long forgotten. Coleman says he remembers his car broke down and while waiting for it to be fixed he figured he'd take in a game, any game. That was what he did as a freelance basketball scout, watch games and assess talent.

It wasn't unusual then for a small, virtually unknown college, always on the edge of bankruptcy, to play games against sports clubs or high schools. Coleman had seen a few, but he'd never spotted a potential recruit, until he saw Harlem Joe Havey score fifty-five of his teams seventy-two points in a romp over the Newark team. Coleman came back to watch a few more games.

It took all the persuasion he could gather but Coleman managed to secure an athletic scholarship for Havey at Western Appalachia College, a small step up in the structure of college sports.

It took one month before Joe decided to quit. He found out that he really did have to study here if he was going to be allowed to play ball. He went back to Harlem, joined his Dad in a smoky bar, and played sax. His mother literally pulled Joe off the stage by his ear, to the roar of the crowd high on a variety of weeds and alcohol. With the money she had stashed away for emergencies, she rode with Joe on a bus back to school, set him down, yelled at him until she was hoarse, then knelt down and cried.

Fortunately she didn't take away Joe's saxophone because it gave him an opportunity to earn pocket money. There wasn't much he wanted to study, but he did want to play ball, and Appalachia had a baseball team and a football team. He tried out for all the sports and made all the teams. Trouble is, there simply wasn't enough time to practice for all the teams, hit the books, and play saxophone. But since the school only had three coaches, who shared coaching duties for all the sports, and Joe was talented at any and every position he played, they let him come to practice whenever he could, and play in whatever game was most important or convenient for Joe. But Joe still hated to study and his playing privileges were suspended until he could improve his grades

Western Appalachia wasn't even affiliated with any national amateur association in those days, so the games they managed to find rarely had anyone from a major league or big time college scouting for talent, except, again for Warner Coleman. Using a contact he had from his own days as an amateur athlete of some note, Coleman managed to get Joe into a small school called North Dakota Forestry, a school that played in a league of some note in the upper Midwest.

It was like a foreign land to Joe: miles of empty land, small towns of wooden buildings, farms, silos, cold wind blowing down from Canada, and so far from Harlem that he wasn't sure how he'd ever get back. Of course, that was the point. Coleman was more interested in Joe's athletic ability, but he sympathized with the mother's wishes. So they decided to send him far enough away from home so he would, they hoped, stay put and get an education while maintaining his eligibility.

Edging off second base Joe heard the blare of a horn in the stands, some fan who needed to make noise. It was a grating sound, yet it briefly reminded him of his saxophone, which he lugged to

45

North Dakota only to discover that hardly anyone there had ever heard of jazz.

No matter, Joe was determined not to make his mother cry again so that meant studying hard until he could get a degree, any degree. In the meantime he played football and basketball and this time he was noticed. In a league championship game he led the North Dakota Forestry Wolves to a 40-7 romp, accounting for most of the points by scoring three touchdowns on runs and one on a pass reception, and kicking the extra points and three field goals. Oh, yeah, he also threw one touchdown pass.

And here I am on second base, finishing a baseball career. Funny how things changed. I loved football, but man it was hard on the body. I think I'd be a cripple by now if I kept playing football.

Joe attracted the attention of the pros and in his first season won the rookie-of-the year award. He was injured in practice before the next season started and had to sit it out. Once he got healthy he was eager for any kind of sports activity and couldn't wait for football season to start again. So he went to the Continental League open tryouts. His baseball skills were raw, but the potential was immense. He was immediately offered a contract by four of the league's teams. But he was still committed to football, though he had promised he'd only play five years. Then he'd get a real job.

Despite his all-star status the next four seasons, Joe did as he had promised and quit football, his aching knees already beginning to make him feel like an old man. Had his mother still been alive he might have kept the promise he made to her to quit sports, get a regular job, and start a family. The family part was already in order, but when his mother passed away, Joe forgot the idea of a job outside of sports. Not quite yet, he said, not while I'm still young.

He was already twenty-eight years old when he began playing baseball in the Continental League. He was an immediate star. One can only speculate what he might have accomplished had he made baseball his primary sport when he was younger, and had his knees been in better shape once he took up a baseball career. Comparisons to Mickey Mantle were obvious.

Joe glanced at Bill Brick, gave the first base coach one more look for a sign, took another step closer towards third base, and saw Sevan kick dirt with his left foot. The count was one and one. Joe took another step towards third.

Sevan never makes a move that doesn't mean something does he, thought Joe. Though he does seem to be taking his sweet time pitching to Keough. Joe watched the catcher as he flashed his fingers, trying to see if any of those movements were telling. Something he remembered from a game somewhere back, maybe a year ago, maybe ten, made him turn ever so slightly to see where Brick was. He caught a movement and without thinking Joe dived back to the safety of second base.

"Safe!" the umpire cried.

"Oh, man, we had him," grumbled Brick.

Havey stood up, dusted himself off, and glanced into the dugout, afraid he'd be removed for a pinch runner.

Brick grinned at Havey and threw the ball back to Sevan. "We had ya, Joe."

"Tie goes to the runner," Havey said, as he took a short lead off the base, trying to show he wasn't cowed by the near pickoff.

At first base, Ben Train sidled back to the bag, reminded that Sevan was one of the best at picking runners off first base.

"Be alert," the first base coach said to Train, as if he needed to be told.

Ben Train was a steady, versatile player, a catcher who could hit for high average and ran better than most practitioners of the tools of ignorance. His claim to fame was winning the batting title three seasons back. He'd been second three other times and was proud of his consistency. He had gone up to bat this inning determined to get on base, after the walk to Havey, to keep a last ditch rally going.

Sevan was tough, but Ben believed it was sheer determination that had enabled him to connect on one of Jack's curves. If I could concentrate that well every time I come up to bat, I could hit .400, Ben pondered. In what league I'm not sure, but I might get a chance in the American or National; have to see what they offer.

"Ball two," Umpire Bailey said.

Train glanced at his coach, lipped, "Anything?"

The coach shook his head. "Just be careful. C'mon Dak!"

Ben took his lead, eyeing Sevan carefully. Don't get picked off Train, don't get picked off, make getting the hit wasted. Sevan threw and Ben eyed the batter as he moved a few feet away from the base. He saw Keough's eyes widen as he began his swing. Ben made ready to dash to second. Havey saw the pitch as it moved towards the plate and thought for sure this ball was going to be put into play.

But the ball broke away sharply and the thud of it hitting Steve Drake's mitt and the swish of Keough's bat hitting nothing but air brought cheers from the crowd. Drake rose up quickly and fired the ball to Don Sandusky, the Jet's first baseman. Train, by instinct, had

48

stepped lively back to first as soon as he realized Keough hadn't connected.

"Don't swat me, Don, I'm not going anywhere--yet," he said.

Both Train and Havey took leads a step less than they'd been taking, miffed that they needed to, in effect accepting that the Jets' pickoff moves had accomplished what they wanted. A shorter lead could be just enough to get the force at second, or an out at home. I hope Joe's knees hold up if he needs to run hard. Wonder why Smithy doesn't put in a runner?

It dawned on Joe Havey that he was actually glad his athletic career was coming to and end. He had already accepted a job as athletic director for the Northern Association of Colleges, beginning in a few weeks. He knew he'd miss the excitement and camaraderie of sports, but he also knew his knees couldn't take much more abuse. And with two youngsters at home it was time to settle down. Maybe a score this game, maybe a chance to play in the last league championship, and that'll be it, adios amigos.

Now the count was full and Havey and Train dared to stretch their leads a bit. Third base looked farther away than it used to, Havey mused. I'm sure they haven't moved it, have they? Sevan fired and Keough smacked the ball into the dirt, foul ball. Happens every time, three and two, big pitch coming, foul ball, do it again.

Ben looked at Sevan, Sevan looked at the batter, and then covered his face with his glove. Ben swore it looked like Jack was smiling, or was it a signal? Keough asked for time, the fans booed, and Ben stepped back to the base.

Everyone repeated themselves: the pitcher took his position on the mound, stared at his catcher who may or may not have been giving a real sign, the fans began to hoot and holler, the coaches bent down with their hands on their knees, the fielders similarly took their defensive positions, the batter moved dirt around and set himself in the batter's box, and the runners took their leads.

Ben was not too surprised by the soft toss from Sevan to Sandusky. He half expected it and knew it was meant to irritate the batter, because Keough got irritated by stuff like that. It's not just a game of brawn, it's a mind game, too.

Okay, everybody do it again. The buzz returned and twenty thousand and some odd number of people rose up yelling and whistling and clapping their hands. Havey edged away from safety, extending his lead a bit more than he had on the last couple of pitches. He glanced around to be sure neither the shortstop nor the second baseman was sneaking close to the bag. Train on first took his lead, a moderate one; he knew he wasn't going anywhere unless Havey was able to advance. Sevan stretched and threw.

THE CATCHER

STEVE DRAKE had been the regular catcher for the Jets for twelve seasons. He had been a major cog in the middle of the 'Golden Years' of the Jets, although the team had won several titles while the great Gene Flood was the first string catcher. Flood had given up the job reluctantly when his knees couldn't take it anymore. He hadn't been a great hitter, so the only job for him now was to become the backup to the young kid, a job he hated. He'd retired soon after and Drake had caught nearly every Jets game since, occasionally resting the second game of a doubleheader.

Like his predecessor, Drake was not a great hitter. He had his moments, but his odd batting stance kept him from developing into the next Johnny Bench. As a kid, Drake was fascinated by the batting stance of the great Cardinal, Stan Musial, with his peek around the shoulder style. But Stan Musial was unique, as testified by his lifetime batting average of .331 and his 475 home runs. Drake would never come close to those figures.

No matter what the coaches tried, Steve felt uncomfortable when they changed his stance, so he continued to copy Stan The Man. Not that he was an automatic out. He was good for a dozen homers or so each season, and once he actually led the league in average until the last week of the season, when a zero for twelve drought killed his chance of a batting title.

His forte was handling pitchers and throwing out base runners. He had a strong, accurate arm and was helped by a staff of pitchers who did a better than average job of keeping the runners close. No one picked off more runners than Steve Drake. His finest moment came in the final game of the season thirty-five Championship Series. The Jets and the Texans were tied three games apiece, and the Jets led in the ninth inning of the seventh game, 4-3, with the tying run on third base.

The pitch was slightly inside, making it a full count on the batter when Drake fired the ball to third base, the throw so close to the batter's face he felt the breeze. The base runner, unfortunately, was Ed Jensen, younger brother of the Jets' manager. He was a bit nonchalant even as the coach yelled in desperation. Ed was picked off for the final out. A stunned crowd was silent for several seconds until they realized what had happened. Steve had immediately glanced into the dugout and saw the sadness on the face of Frank Jensen.

Drake stood and gave Umpire Archie Bailey a dirty look, but he knew the last pitch to Joe Havey, who now stood on second base, having been sent there by the single by the next batter, Ben Train, had been outside, ball four without a doubt. But he was upset and there was no one else to glare at. He looked at Frank Jensen in the dugout and saw that he was in turn staring at the pitcher.

Johnny isn't warmed up yet, Steve thought; takes him longer these days. What the hell's Jack doing out there? Steve turned to Bailey, who nodded, and trotted out towards the mound.

"What the hell you doin', Jack?"

"Oh, I was wondering if I should enter the draft or not. What're you gonna do?"

"God, man, not now. We got the winning run coming to bat! Get your mind straight!"

Sevan laughed. "You're so serious, Stevie! Rest easy; now, we gonna start Dak the usual way?"

"Sure. He'll be looking for it, but you put it where I ask and we'll get him. Now let's go. I'll flash some signs just to give Havey something to look at, but you know what to give me."

Drake crouched behind the plate and flashed his fingers. These signs meant nothing because the catcher knew what Sevan was going to throw. Jack shook his head as if in disagreement with Drake's suggestion of pitches.

I don't think we're fooling anyone, the catcher thought, but what the hell. Drake gave a false target, setting his glove in the middle of the plate, belt high to the batter, Dakota Keough, the Cowboys' clean-up hitter. He waited while Jack Sevan took longer than usual. Maybe he knows he's getting tired and wants to give Johnny more time to get ready. He seems distracted and Drake felt a spasm of worry.

He was startled and almost missed the ball when it came in high and over the center of the plate. He had already moved his glove inside, where the pitch was supposed to be, and had to move back to grab it. Keough was so surprised that he was late in his swing and was only able to hit a long foul ball that sliced into the stands.

Drake called "Time", and ran to the mound.

"You okay? Are we on the same page?" Drake asked Sevan.

Jack stared at his catcher and for a second Steve thought Jack was angry with him. Jack and Drake had pitched and caught too many games together to argue now.

"Yeah, yeah, sorry. I'm fine. The usual script, Stevie."

"You know, Johnny's almost warm, if you want him."

Jack's angry glare was his answer and Drake turned without another word and retreated to his position behind the plate.

"You guys trying to throw me off, Steve?" asked Dakota Keough, a smile in his voice and on his face. He stepped back and gripped his bat, looking at it as if it could tell him where the hits were.

"We'll talk later Dak, let's go," Drake replied curtly.

Like a lot of battery mates, Jack and Steve had become close, not just as ball players but as friends. Yes, most of their conversation had to do with pitching--how to pitch this batter or that batter, do we handle him the same way all the time or change our pattern occasionally. With Keough they didn't change much. Not that he wasn't dangerous, but he was predictable. It was true, as announcers had advised fans forever, that control was the key to success on the mound.

The intimacy of their friendship had taken beatings over the years because of Jack's marital problems. He'd try to discuss issues with Steve that the latter did not want to hear about. When Jack was married, at least when he was happily married, the two couples frequently socialized in the off-season. When things were going bad, it threw cold water on the relationships.

Someone not familiar with Jack's personal life could tell there had been problems by looking at his pitching statistics. In the first year of Jack's first marriage, he was only 9-7, probably due to the more joyous distractions of marriage. The next three years, as he settled into a happy life style, he was nearly unhittable. Then the marriage fizzled, his earned run average soared, and Steve Drake's job of handling his pitching staff became tougher. Drake's batting average tumbled and the Jets had their worst season in history. The second marriage showed a statistical repeat.

Fortunately, after Jack's second divorce, he recovered quicker and once again had settled into his role as the most effective pitcher in the league. Steve hated to even suggest that Jack avoid women until he retired from pitching, but he and everyone on the team hoped he would.

Let's go Jack, Steve said, too softly for anyone to hear. Jack's second pitch missed the right edge of the plate by a fraction of an inch. Steve thought they'd get the call, a real break since this pitch hadn't been calculated to be a strike, but Bailey let it go. Drake stood up and once more gave Bailey a nasty glare, and the umpire looked down at his counter, avoiding Drake's stare in a way that said, I may have missed that one, but it was close so don't give me any grief.

Drake watched Sevan wander around the mound while rubbing the ball. He saw him kick a clod of dirt with his left foot. The catcher lifted his mask to better view the situation. A slight nod from Bill Brick at second base said that he'd seen the signal.

Drake crouched once Sevan appeared ready. He gave the sign that meant everyone was on board; it was just a matter of how long a lead Havey took off second. Drake would decide; if Havey stayed close, there was no sense in trying a play that didn't have any chance to succeed, and he'd signal to call off the pickoff attempt. The catcher watched Harlem Joe take his lead, his eyes hidden by the mask. The runner stretched his lead and Drake made ready for the pitch.

Just as Jack turned to make his throw Havey, as if a bird sitting on his shoulder had whispered to him, began to inch back towards the base. As he saw the pitcher's move he dove for the bag.

"Safe!" the umpire cried.

"Oh, man, we had him," grumbled Brick.

Would have been nice, Drake thought. He got into position quickly. Standard procedure for the Jets was that after such a play the pitcher, whoever he was, would hurry the next pitch, the idea being to catch the batter and runners before they were completely ready.

The pitch came in and hit Drake's glove exactly where he'd placed it, three inches outside. The batter wouldn't bite. "Ball two," Umpire Bailey said, to no one's surprise.

Drake tossed the ball back to Sevan. Okay, we're where we expected to be, two and one. And, both runners have cut their lead by a few inches, maybe just enough to make a difference. Games and pennants have been won and lost by less than a few inches. Don't I know it, the catcher recollected.

Season twenty-nine, I remember it well. We were going for three straight. We had Mike Williams one and two, a great position to be in. the next pitch was there, I swear it was, right on the black, a change up that froze Williams. But Lester, he was the plate umpire that day, he didn't call it. I almost got thrown out just for the look I gave him.

Johnny was in then, Johnny the great game saver. But even he wasn't immune to defeat when you aren't getting the calls on the close ones. The next pitch was nearly as close and with two strikes Williams figured he better not push his luck. He swung and hit a high fly, not one of those exploding line drives he usually hit that kept rising like a rocket until it hit something, usually the facade of the upper deck. No, this was a towering pop fly that kept floating out to left field, barely fair. The left fielder, Robinson it was then, was standing at the wall waiting, like for a bus, it took so long for the ball to come down. Robinson climbed the fence, reached back, and had the ball hit the top of his glove before it fell down, in slow motion, into the hands of fan, a game winning home run. Inches. Knocked us out of it and the Texans went on the win the League Championship. Inches, man, inches.

As Steve prepared for the next pitch his peripheral vision caught the runner on first, Ben Train, getting greedy again. Sevan's next pitch also scared Drake as for a heartbeat it looked like it too, like the first pitch in the sequence, would be too good to give Keough. Then, worrywart, the ball broke away sharply and Keough's bat made a swishing sound as it hit nothing but air.

Drake didn't take time to think about the call as he whipped the ball to first baseman Don Sandusky, seriously trying for a pickoff. It was close, but not nearly enough. I had to try, Drake thought; Jack needs to watch him a little more.

Again Sevan seemed to take more time than usual. What the hell in the good goddamn is going on with him?! Just as Drake rose up from his crouch, getting irritated with his pitcher's dawdling, Sevan got set. The catcher hunched down and gave the signal—outside and low, nowhere near where Keough can reach it, and if he does, the best he'll do is bounce an easy hopper to Brick at second base.

The pitch was where Drake wanted it, even if it did set up a full count. Sevan had control coveted by every pitcher in the league, and Drake never feared going to three balls on a batter. Yet, Jack does seem to be a little off lately. His mind is not all here for some reason. Yeah, we've all been a little taken aback with the news. We knew it was coming long ago; the party's over. No one wanted to accept the fact that this was it, our league, our livelihood, the friendships and the rivalries; not to mention a regular paycheck. To talk about it will make

57

it reality, but if we ignore the inevitable it will go away and we can continue on as before. It's gnawing at all of us.

The crowd began to stir more and more as the climax of the at bat, and the game itself, came nearer with each pitch. People stood cheering and yelling and clapping. You can't win the Championship too many times, and if this is the end of the league, the Jets' fans wanted to go out a winner. Don't we all, don't we all.

Drake checked the defense. He knew Jensen was constantly on the defensive setup, but it's hard to note everyone's position on every pitch. If it's going to be an inside pitch, the third baseman and the leftfielder may want to shade over to the line. But, if the pitch isn't on target, it could end up in the gap. Ce la vie.

Drake gazed at the crowd, realizing he might not ever be in this position again. "Quite a sight, isn't it?" he said, not expecting an answer.

The umpire took off his mask. "What are you looking at, Steve?"

"That," the catcher gestured. "The crowd. Listen to them."

"Oh, hell," said Keough, "that ain't nothin'. You ever been to Yankee Stadium?"

"Let's go," said Bailey.

The pitch was right where Drake wanted it, and right where Keough expected it to be. He only got a tiny piece of the ball, just hard enough that the catcher couldn't hold on to it. The ball trickled away in the dirt as Keough cursed.

A year or two ago Keough would have never touched that ball, but even Jack has lost a little, Drake reflected. We're lucky Dak didn't smash that one all the way to downtown.

Everyone got into their places again, a re-set, as if they had marks on a stage to show where they should stand, cue cards to tell them what to say. Again Sevan took his time. For a moment he covered his face with his glove and Drake thought Jack was laughing. Keough called time and stepped out.

Drake knew what Jack would do now, even if it wasn't serious. Sure enough, just when Keough was all set, deep in concentration, his mind on nothing but what he was going to do to that little white ball, Sevan lobbed a toss to first, as if playing catch. Just something to screw with Keough's mental state.

Keough shook his head, stepped back and asked for time. He kicked at the dirt in the batter's box until he had moved it around and probably back to where it was before he started. Drake smiled behind his mask and nonchalantly touched the side of the mask. His gut told him a change in the normal progression of pitches was needed.

The buzz began again and twenty thousand and some odd number of people rose up yelling and whistling and clapping their hands. The base runners edged away from safety, Joe Havey extending his lead a bit more than he had on the last couple of pitches. Ben Train on first took a moderate lead; he knew he wasn't going anywhere unless Havey was able to advance. Sevan waited patiently for Keough to get in the box, and when the batter was set, he stretched and threw.

THE RIGHT FIELDER

AL LUCKY pounded his fist into his glove, something he and every other outfielder had done countless times, for no other reason than it felt good. The glove's almost as old as me, Lucky thought, getting ready for one more catch, one more ball to set down easily into the pocket, another out safely secure.

Al Lucky *was* the Jets. More so than Jack Sevan, more so than Frank Jensen, or Ken Phillips, the speedy centerfielder, who covered more ground than Patton's army had at the Battle of the Bulge. More so, except for those who remembered the earliest days of the league and the Polak, Johnny Olzsewski. Johnny O. held all the league home run and slugging records until Mike Williams and Lucky came along. Young studs then, the two would battle like McGwire and Sosa did in 1998, but they did it nearly every season.

Lucky was just as proud of his defensive records. In the first few years of his career he always led the league in outfield assists. His arm was a bazooka and time and again he shocked base runners who couldn't believe he could throw so far, and so accurately. Finally they quit running on him and he seldom was tested. A few times he took it easy in pre-game warm-ups, trying to make it look like his arm was tired or sore. A runner or two bit and Lucky zapped them, and after that he couldn't fool anybody. It was a good thing, too, because now his arm really was getting tired. Before the season began Al knew this was the end of the line, but he hadn't announced his retirement, and once the rumors about the death of the League came true, he didn't have to.

He rubbed his right elbow now, which had been slightly sore ever since he had to slide into third base three games ago. His elbow had bounced off the ground and had ached on and off. Fortunately he hadn't had to make any long or hard throws since then.

Al Lucky had hoped to coach for a while and then take over for Jensen. Now all he could hope for would be a minor league slot for one of the American or National League teams. He didn't think he'd care for the minors. Call me snobbish, but I've been playing in the big tent for too long to go back to bumpy bus rides between dusty towns where McDonald's is gourmet dining. Besides, he wanted to be home more, with Suzie and the kids.

Lucky had come up the same year as Jack Sevan, who was standing back of the mound now, rubbing the baseball and apparently studying the scoreboard. Al was Rookie-of-the Year, Sevan was erratic, and shuffled back and forth to the minors before he found his control. So it was the next season before Al came to know Jack. As they both developed into potent players, they led the Jets to an amazing run of six championships in the next eight seasons.

They slumped for several seasons afterwards, no coincidence that this was when Jack was going through a divorce and Al had lost his wife in a car accident. Al had been so distraught he left the team and drove aimlessly for a week, scaring his relatives, friends, and of course, the team. He was recognized in a coffee shop and a fan showed him a newspaper story that said Al Lucky was missing and it was feared he had taken his life. He called the team but said he wasn't ready to come back. They could fire him if they wanted to.

Back at home, a month later, listening to the Jets' game on radio Al realized he hadn't done anything, not even opened the mail, since Jenny had died. He felt worse now than he did at the funeral. Sitting here drinking beer and listening to my teammates lose games is not going to bring Jenny back, he realized, as if he and he alone was able to comprehend that shocking truth. As if no one else had ever lost a loved one.

Al returned to the team, batted .215 with four home runs the rest of the way and the Jets tumbled in the standings. Even the traditionally riotous and tense games with their arch rivals, the Texans, lost their luster as the team of Mike Williams and Frank Ford romped to three titles in the next four seasons.

Al met Suzie at a late season game against the Texans. She was Mike William's sister-in-law and was watching the game with Williams' wife. Al knew Mike's wife and when he noticed a gorgeous brunette sitting next to her he was so fascinated he was called out on three pitches without taking the bat off his shoulder. Fortunately for him the Jets were twelve games out of first place and going nowhere. The next time he came up to bat he was taken out for a pinch-hitter for the first and only time in his career.

After the game he and a few players from both teams went to dinner, as this had been the final game of the season against the Texans. Mike Williams had set a new league home run record the prior season, and was on track to break his own record this season, so he was feeling generous towards his slugging rival.

"Meet Sheila's sister, Al, Suzie, from the Augusta area."

If it wasn't love at first sight, it was soon after.

I wonder what Jack's doing, taking so long, Al wondered. He saw the catcher saunter to the mound to find out the same thing. Funny, Al thought, how Jack and I both lost wives at about the same time, he to a divorce, me to an accident, yet we both recovered to have our best years in baseball. He seemed to thrive once he was single again, whereas I put it together after I met Suzie.

The next five seasons Al Lucky went on a hitting tear the likes of which the league had never seen, nor would see. He destroyed the season home run record with 53 round trippers, and would break the fifty-homer mark three seasons in a row. He won the home run and runs batted in titles five years out of six, cementing his place in the Continental League Hall of Fame. Even this season, his last, had been decent, and Al felt it was a good one to go out on. He never wanted to get to the point Jack had come to, where the game meant so much his family got lost in the shuffle. He could hardly wait to have more time with the kids.

Sevan was finally ready to pitch and Lucky reminded himself of the situation. Two on, one out, we've got a two run lead, and Havey's on second. I can't believe he'd try to score on me if Dak drops one in here, little does he know he might make it with my arm at less than its best.

He was surprised by the long, loud foul that flew into the stands. I didn't think Jack would give him anything he could get wood on. Al watched as the catcher, Steve Drake, trotted out to the mound again. Obviously they need to get straight on their strategy with Keough.

Al took a quick glance to the box seats in back of the Jets' dugout. Suzie was there, she usually was, but with the kids growing there were some games she couldn't make. But this one, the last game of the regular season, she wouldn't miss. I always love to see her in her regular seat.

Don't I distract you, she'd once asked. No, baby, not being there is the distraction. Did you know the statistician figured out that my batting average, home runs, and runs batted in are twenty-five percent higher when you are at the games? Suzie had waved him off as if she knew he was pulling her league, but it was true, proven mathematically. Today, however, had been a bust; nothing but a bleeding single. Still, we're ahead.

Al saw a signal from Frank Jensen and he moved a few feet to his left. Okay, Frank, I don't think Dak can slice this far over and keep it fair, but you're the boss. As he set himself he saw movement near the area where Suzie was sitting, and saw Mike Williams and his wife, Suzie's sister, move in. Al smiled to see Williams. He and Mike had some great duels over the years. Poor sucker, gets hurt, this, the last season.

Kind off ironic, Al thought, that after either Mike or I always led the league in homers and RBIs, this last season he gets hurt enough to sit him down, I miss twenty some games because of injuries, and neither one of us is going to win any slugging awards.

Al watched Jack's sudden throw to second, thought they had Havey, and pounded his glove in frustration when the umpire called him safe. Brick appeared to argue, but not much. He glanced again at the box seats, caught Suzie's eyes and smiled when she waved at him and pointed to Mike and his wife, Sheila. Al nodded, and when Mike waved Al raised his glove slightly in response.

The count went to two and one and Al got his mind into gear. He was always in the game, but in certain situations, depending on the batter, the count, the score, other variables, he was more or less engrossed. That was why he had been so surprised that Keough had gotten a crack at the first pitch. Now the count was two and one, closer to where something had to happen, assuming Jack doesn't get the strike out, which I'm sure he would love. Keough doesn't usually hit to right, but he has at times, and with Jack obviously tiring, he might leave one hanging on the outside corner.

Al Lucky watched Keough take a big swing and cut only air. The crowd cheered, sensing, or at least wishing, for the kill. They want us in one more, one final Championship Series as much as we do, maybe more.

Al remembered back to the first Championship Series after he and Suzie had gotten married. Sure enough, they were up against the Texans, a team that had won the season series from the Jets. Suzie sat behind the Jets' dugout, cheering for Al, while her sister sat behind the Texans' dugout, cheering for her husband. Trouble is, Suzie would also cheer when Mike got a hit, and Sheila would cheer when Al got a hit.

The first game of the series went into the ninth inning tied 3-3. Williams smashed a long drive to right field. Al backed up to the fence, and at the last split second kicked up on the fence with his right foot and caught the ball. Suzie cheered, of course, and Sheila started to clap for Al's great catch, until she realized to her embarrassment that it was an out against her husband's team. Afterwards, the wives decided that when the Jets and the Texans played they'd best cheer only for their respective husband's team. It was easier that way. But this might be the first time the star of the Texans was sitting on the Jets' side of the field, rooting along with the hometown fans despite a spattering of boos as some of the fans recognized Williams.

The count went full. Al moved a few feet towards center. He looked towards the dugout and saw Jensen glance his way, signing nothing, approving Al's position. He looked towards the Cowboy's dugout, wondering if at the last they'd send in a runner for Havey. Man, I love to catch the ball, but a nice, easy, ground ball double play would be wonderful here.

He was set, everybody was set, the crowd was going nuts, cowbells were ringing, horns were tooting, and Al Lucky knew he was going to miss this. You can watch the games, you can coach the games, but there ain't nothing like being here, being ready to catch the ball, fire it in, nail the runner. Sometimes I think I enjoy playing outfield more than I do batting. The pitch came and Keough smacked the ball into the ground and Al got the impression he was actually trying to hit it to right. Even way out in right field Al could hear Keough's curse. Lucky understood the hitter's frustration of not clobbering a pitch he felt he should have handled.

Everybody got ready again. But Sevan wasn't ready. He stood on the mound, his glove covering his mouth. What the hell, is he sick, or what? Dakota Keough asked for time, got it, and stepped out of the batter's box. Some fans booed, the hometown crowds blaming Keough for stalling. Al thought Sevan was laughing.

Al chuckled to himself because he thought he knew what Jack found so funny in this situation. Thinking back to that time with Williams when Jack almost fell off the mound he was laughing so hard. Al looked at the grass, reached down and pulled a few blades and threw them up, ostensibly to check the wind. But often pulling blades of grass was just something outfielders did between pitches, for no good reason at all.

Sevan set and threw to first, just to remind the runner he hadn't forgotten about him. Keough shook his head, stepped back and asked for time, or anyway he stepped out as if his request was automatically approved. He kicked at the dirt in the batter's box until he had moved it around and probably back to where it was before he started his landscaping.

The buzz began again and twenty thousand people rose up yelling and whistling and clapping their hands. Al caught a wag of the fingers from the first baseman, Don Sandusky. Yeah, Sands the "hot shot", how wrong I was. The runners took their lead, the fielders got into their crouching position. Jack Sevan went into his stretch and fired.

THE INFIELDERS

DON SANDUSKY whacked Ben Train on the leg with his glove.

"Don't swat me, Don, I'm not going anywhere--yet," said Train who had smartly hopped back onto the bag as Drake snapped the throw.

Sandusky smirked and tossed the ball back to Sevan.

Sandusky was having one of those 'Fountain of Youth' seasons, leading the league in home runs and RBIs, categories that had been the sole property of Al Lucky and/or Mike Williams for as long as some folks could remember. It was considerable satisfaction for Sandusky, who had burst onto the Continental League scene as a major star, and had stayed a major star, but had nearly always had to take a back seat to the Jets' mega-hero, Al Lucky. And if Lucky wasn't leading the league in all the slugging categories, Williams of the Texans was.

True, Williams had missed half the season with injuries and Lucky nearly twenty-five games, but still, it wasn't bad for one of the old-timers. In fact, Jensen himself had said to Don, after he hit a two-run homer in the first inning of today's game, "Way to go, Sands, keep it in the family."

Sandusky had amazed the league when as a rookie he led the Explorer's to the title, winning Rookie-of-the-Year honors, along with leading in most of the power statistics. The Explorers thought they were now in position to challenge for league dominance, but for a variety of reasons, mostly lack of consistent pitching, it didn't happen.

So they packaged Sandusky to the Jet's for an aging ace and several young pitchers, hoping for one quick season of glory.

There was immediate tension in the Jets' locker room when Sandusky arrived, like a cloud of old smoke that hugs the ceiling and leaves a stale odor, worst than the odor of old gym socks that have sat in the corner for three weeks.

Jensen had batted third in the Jets' lineup, Al Lucky cleanup. When Sandusky became a Jet the lineup was revised, with Lucky moving to third and Sandusky to cleanup, Jensen dropping to fifth. The older superstar, Jensen, and the current and future superstar, Lucky, weren't happy.

In Sandusky's first game with the Jets they faced the Texans on the road. The first two batters singled off Frank Ford and Lucky patiently worked a walk. As Lucky related later, as he trotted to first base he thought, OK, hot shot, let's see what you can do against Ford with the bags loaded.

Frank Ford was to Jack Sevan what Phil Mickleson was to Tiger Woods. A great pitcher in his own right, he generally had to stand slightly in the shadow of Sevan. To his credit, Ford lost a lot more close games than Sevan had, the latter the beneficiary of the greatest "murderers row" anyone had ever seen, once Lucky-Sandusky-Jensen accepted their places in the batting order. Ford topped Sevan in some categories: he had four no-hitters to Sevan's three, and he only gave up one grand slam homer in all his career.

It came on the first pitch to Sandusky in his first at bat for the Jets. Sandusky tried not to smirk as he rounded the bases, but it was difficult. Lucky greeted him at the plate with, "Nice going, hot shot!"

Ford was so mad he struck out thirteen Jets and only gave up one more hit the rest of the game. But he lost, 4-2.

Lucky and Sandusky never became bosom buddies, but they were cooperative teammates and respected each other's abilities. Sandusky accepted the fact that he would never be *the* main man of the Jets, and Lucky acknowledged that he probably got more good pitches to hit than he would if the batter following him had been anyone less potent than Sandusky. Every time Lucky got a pumpkin to hit with men on base, and belted it for a homer, Sandusky would tease him, "You owe me!"

Jensen's runs batted in totals suffered thereafter but he never complained that with Al and Don batting ahead of him, the bases were usually clean. That was one hundred percent true, but as long as the Jets kept winning, no one cared too much who produced the most runs.

A few seasons later the Jets brought up a young first baseman who could hit the ball a mile, when he did hit it. Sandusky stayed in the outfield but eventually moved to first base when the legs couldn't deal with line drives in the gap. Lucky still kidded him because Al was two years older than Don, and still able to cover his ground. The young first baseman, Ron Jackson, tried to learn to play outfield and third base, but for the most part he played the second game of doubleheaders, when Sands needed a break, or was used as a pinch-hitter.

This season, when Lucky was laid down with an injury for several weeks, the Jets slumped. In the fifth inning of a game that would be their fourth loss in a row, Jensen, who seldom moved from his position in the dugout, sauntered over to the bench and sat down next to Sandusky. He sat there for several minutes without saying a word. He picked at something stuck in his teeth, then spat out a dozen or more of some sort of seed.

"I'm thinking of starting Ron at first base for a few games."

"You want me to go the outfield?" Sandusky asked.

"No," Jensen said, and got up and walked away.

In his next at bat Sandusky hit a home run, though it was too late to help in that game.

The next day Sandusky looked at the lineup card and his name was in the usual position as cleanup hitter, playing first base. Sandusky homered again and went on an offensive barrage that led the Jets to an eleven game winning streak and a charge into first place. Today his 38th homer and 94th & 95th runs batted in might just be enough to clinch the division title for the Jets.

Sandusky held Train close and along with thousands of fans waited for Sevan. Everyone waits on the pitcher. The umpire may try to move the game along, but in the end the game waits on the man on the mound. Jack's usually quick, sometimes too quick, but he sure is farting around this inning, Sandusky thought. He saw Jack cover his face with his glove, but could tell from Jack's eyes peeking over the glove, that the damn fool was laughing! What the hell!

Train returned to the bag and looked at Sandusky.

"Jack's got the giggles, or you guys have some new signs."

"Don't ask me, he's one of those weird lefthanders."

Train again took a short lead and hopped back when Sevan turned and tossed the ball to Sandusky. Don tossed it back, positioned himself, and Train again edged off the base. The batter stepped back and asked for time. He kicked at the dirt in the batter's box until he was satisfied with the layout.

Sandusky looked at Sevan, then to Drake, saw him touch the side of his mask. So, eschew the fastball this time. Dak will be surprised. He reached his right hand behind his back and wagged his fingers so the right fielder would know what kind of pitch was coming. He glanced to his right, to check Brick's position near second base, and then set his eyes on the pitcher.

BILL BRICK stood next to second base, his arms folded, waiting for the pitcher and catcher to finish their conference. Next to them, two feet solidly set on top of the bag, stood Joe Havey, the kid from Harlem.

"What are you gonna do, Joe? I mean, after this is over?"

"This is it for me. I'm moving to Idaho, got a job as athletic director for the Northern Association. I can't wait."

Brick shook his head. "Hard to believe, you not playing some kind of ball somewhere."

"Heh, maybe I'll join a softball league. You?"

Brick shrugged. "Don't know for sure. I've got some connections with the Cardinals; I may get a coaching gig."

The catcher was back behind home plate, Sevan on the mound was ready to pitch, and Brick moved to his position while Havey took a lead off the base, watching Brick as warily as if he were a deadly enemy, instead of someone he'd just been having a pleasant conversation with.

After the first pitch Havey extended his lead. The next pitch was ball one and as Brick scuffed at the dirt around his position he noticed a kick by Sevan, as if he was unsatisfied with the condition of the dirt around his mound. He glanced at the catcher, watched Havey as he stepped off the base, another foot or so longer lead than previously.

Bill Brick was yet another of the old-timers who had kept the Jets as the dominant team in the league for many seasons. He was a tough player who didn't get out of the way of any base runner. It was said that he'd throw to first in the face of an oncoming locomotive. If his name hadn't been Brick, he'd have been called that anyway, since opponents said that sliding into him at second base was like crashing into a brick wall.

Brick wasn't a great hitter, but he could scarf up ground balls like a vacuum cleaner. It was an amazing upset when he didn't top all second basemen in fielding percentage. But like most of the Jets, he was feeling his age. For the past two seasons his role had been as much as a fielding coach as a player. Chip Bladoc had taken over as the regular and had performed fairly well. A double play here or there that he hadn't made, that Brick might well have, and the Jets would have a lead that wasn't in jeopardy in this last regularly scheduled game of the season, a local sportswriter and several fans had suggested.

At least that's the scuttlebutt Brick heard, but he didn't agree with the sentiment. He hated to admit that he himself wasn't as quick as he used to be, and hated to think anyone noticed when he was on the field. He felt that the whisperings that he was still a bettor defensive player than Bladoc were out of loyalty more than reality.

But he insisted he get some playing time, to keep from being bored, and to keep his skills fresh for when they were needed. And when it came to one of those so-called "crucial" games, an old hand like Frank Jensen was apt to call on the other old hands he was used to seeing on the field.

Sevan spun and fired the ball towards second base. Brick had to time his move. If he wasn't where the ball was supposed to be, or Sevan didn't throw it to where Brick was going to be, the ball would continue into center field.

Bill Brick moved like a ballerina, but Havey sensed something and began to move back towards the base a split second before Sevan threw. He dived at the bag and touched it just as Brick slapped the tag on him.

"Safe!" the umpire cried.

"Oh, man, we had him," grumbled Brick.

Havey stood up, dusted himself off. Brick grinned at the runner and threw the ball back to Sevan. "We had ya, Joe."

"Tie goes to the runner," Havey said, as he took a short lead off the base, trying to show he wasn't cowed by the near pickoff. But Brick noticed the lead was slightly less than it had been, justifying the pickoff attempt. Havey was no jackrabbit anymore, and one or two steps might make the difference if he tries to score on a hit.

Brick scanned every player on the field, the coaches, and Jensen in the dugout, standing solidly like a statue of some Civil War General, except for an occasional swipe at his mustache. He better be careful some pigeon doesn't set down on his head, a thought that almost brought a grin to the face of the stolid infielder.

The count had gone full and Havey stretched his lead just a bit. Harlem Joe looked towards third and Brick wondered if Joe was estimating how many steps it would take him to get there. Surely one or two more than it used to. Ben checked Drake's movements, fingers picking at a clod of dirt, scratching his thigh, touching his mask. Some of those movements meant something, some didn't. No more pickoff attempts, Brick thought. Jack needs to concentrate on Keough. Get him to pound one into the dirt and we can get two and go have a beer.

Just as everyone seemed ready for what might be the climax of the game, Sevan covered his face with his glove and Ben thought it sure looks like he's laughing. But I don't know what the hell is so funny. Havey inched back a bit towards second base. The batter called time and stepped out.

The players relaxed for a few seconds while a few hundred fans booed, then everyone re-wound themselves, the fans cheering and screaming, the players set in their positions, concentrating on the situation at hand. Sevan tossed the ball to first base.

Keough shook his head, stepped back and asked for time again. The runners returned to their respective bases, touching them, a gesture implying a moment of security, then edged off again.

The buzz returned and twenty thousand and some odd number of people rose up yelling and whistling and clapping their hands.

Brick punched his glove as he glanced at Drake and saw him nonchalantly touched the side of his mask. Brick relayed the sign to the outfield, although Sandusky had probably done so also. Many times it made no difference, but a big league hitter can do different things with a fastball as opposed to a curve, slider, or even a screwball, a pitch few hurlers had in their repertoire. How the defense sets up for a particular pitch may decide whether the hitter gets on base, or is put out because the fielder positioned himself according to the pitch. He looked one more time at Havey, just a bit to get the runner to look back at him and maybe, just maybe, gain a split second for the defense.

On the mound, Jack Sevan went into his motion, his body becoming a pretzel as he twisted and willed it to hurl a round object in a manner the body was not built for, at a speed fast enough it could kill a person if it hit just so. The white round object became a blur.

THE UMPIRE

ARCHIE 'JUGHEAD' BAILEY hated his name, Archibald, didn't much care for Archie, and you can just imagine what he thought of his nickname, 'Jughead', or worse, 'Jugs', as some players called him, including the current batter, Dakota Keough. But for an umpire, a person who is expected to be perfect in his job performance and is strongly criticized when someone thinks he isn't perfect, Jughead was a remarkably even-tempered person who didn't even get mad when he threw you out of the ball game.

"You done, Frank?" he might ask Manager Frank Jensen after Jensen had bitched about a call. Jensen himself was easy-going and calm and didn't yell a lot. So their arguments were so peaceful that the players had been known to laugh at the two.

"Yeah, I'm done, Jughead," Frank would say.

"I asked you not to call me Jughead in front of the players, Frank."

"Well, I don't remember your name."

"It's Arch...never mind, you're outta here," Jughead would say, raising in arm and pointing towards the dugout, but not raising his voice.

"Well, for Pete's Sakes, Jughead (that was cursing for Jensen), what for?"

"Because it's time to end this discussion, Frank, and you won't leave unless I throw you out. Besides, the players won't respect me if I don't throw you out."

"Well that ain't right, Jughead."

"File a complaint, Frank."

And Frank would slowly turn away, stop to say something to any player who was nearby, just to irk Bailey, eventually get to the dugout, walking so slowly you'd think he was about to fall over, take his spot where he usually stood, wait for Bailey to reiterate his 'you're outta here' gesture, then move, very slowly again, down the walkway where he would spend the rest of the game, listening to the noise and getting updates from one of his coaches.

Bailey, like all the other umpires, liked it when Jack Sevan pitched. The games went quickly because that's how Sevan worked. And if he was really on his game, the whole show would be over in less than two hours. This game had moved fairly fast, but a little slow as it progressed because of the importance of the game. Now Sevan was holding things up while he appeared to be daydreaming on the mound.

Bailey waited patiently while the catcher went to talk to Sevan.

"For Christ's sake, Jugs, let's go," the batter, Dakota Keough said.

"A second, Dak."

"They're stalling."

Bailey took off his mask and stepped over home plate, just as Steve Drake began to trot back to his position.

"You guys ready to play ball?" he asked.

"Yessir. Jack's getting nostalgic out there."

Keough fouled off the first pitch, one that had come in much more over the plate than Sevan had intended, giving the batter a ball he might have handled if he hadn't been so surprised by its attractive location.

The catcher called time and ran out to the mound.

"Fuck, Jugs, I shoulda killed that one."

"Shoulda, coulda, woulda," replied the umpire.

Keough grunted.

Everybody's getting a little pissy, Bailey thought. The league is going under, the players are getting older, and the day's getting hotter. Every pitch can make the difference between who wins and loses, who goes to the Championship Series, who goes home; how many times had he heard that?

But an umpire can't care about who wins and who loses. All he can care about is making the call, and making it right. Of course I know this game decides which of these teams stays alive. How could I not know, though sometimes I wish I didn't.

Bailey couldn't help but recall how well Sevan had handled Keough in today's game. The tendency might then be to believe that if the pitch is close to a strike, and the batter doesn't swing, it must be a strike, right, because this pitcher knows how to handle this batter. But you can't think that way, you have to put it out of your mind and call the game as if it's always the first batter in the first game of the season, nothing much on the line.

The second pitch came in and Bailey made his instantaneous decision, which in this case was to *not* call a strike, thus, after the briefest of hesitations, he mumbled "Ball one".

Steve Drake, the veteran catcher turned his head and gave Bailey a dirty look. Don't say anything, Steve, Bailey thought to himself. You guys know I don't want to throw anybody out of this game so don't do or say anything.

Most games were the same, in a sense. Balls and strikes, safe and out, and most calls were easy to make, obvious to anybody except a batter in a slump who believes every pitch he doesn't swing at is three feet outside. But even an umpire has feelings. Bailey and his fellow umps had talked before the game about their own futures. For most of them it wouldn't be hard to get jobs somewhere. They were versatile, able to umpire at all levels of baseball, and referee basketball and football. But Bailey knew he'd missed the league.

He'd umpired in the National and American Leagues for two seasons and as a substitute several times. It was more serious, more argumentative than the Continental League. I guess there's more at stake; more money, anyway. He didn't like it so he opted for a career in the Continental League for less pay, but less headaches, less travel time and more time at home. He made up some of the difference in income by umpiring college and high school games. It was a decent living.

What did frost him was that people thought it was so easy to be an umpire. Yeah, you try calling balls and strike when the ball is speeding in at 90 or more miles per hour, some guy is swinging at it, or the ball breaks from in to out, or up to down, or the batter starts his swing then tries to stop, and will swear to holy heaven that he held up, and you have to watch for balks, you have to be aware of foul tips, catcher's or batter's interference, fair or foul calls, and keep track of the count and the outs; it ain't that damn easy, folks.

And the language some of these guys use! My mother would die, *I* want to die sometimes because I want to let them have their say, vent a bit, show that they know they are right and an innocent victim of the blind bat umpire's incompetence. Oy vey!

Bailey was ready for the next pitch when Sevan whirled and threw to second base. It was close, but Lester got it right, safe. Nice try, Jack. The umpire reset himself, eyed Sevan, glanced at where Drake held his glove, a little outside, which would make it easy to call this pitch if it hit its target, then returned his attention to the pitcher.

The ball came in and hit Drake's glove exactly where he'd placed it, three inches outside. The batter didn't bite. "Ball two," Bailey said. No argument there, just a setup pitch, a teaser by Sevan, hoping Keough would bite on a pitch he likely couldn't hit well.

The next pitch was a temptation and Keough took a big swing, an overeager swing. The thud of the ball hitting the catcher's mitt and the swish of the bat hitting nothing but air brought cheers from the crowd.

"Fuckin' A," gasped Keough, who spat in the dirt and didn't notice that Drake had whipped the ball to first trying for a pickoff.

"Steerike!" called Bailey.

The catcher zipped the ball to first, trying for a pickoff, to no avail. Sevan got the ball back but again took more time than usual.

"We're gonna be here all day, Jugs. Sevan can't decide what he wants to do," Keough said.

"What, you got a hot date?"

Keough laughed and Drake, who had stood up and began to move out to the mound, got back into his crouch.

"Get ready, Dak, I don't want you to say you weren't ready."

"Bring it on, Stevie."

The pitch was outside and low, and the batter showed no interest. Bailey didn't say anything, the pitch was obviously not a strike, but indicated with raised fingers, three on one hand, two on the other, that we have a full count, though surely everyone knew.

The crowd was starting to get into it now, ninth inning, full count, and their home team two outs away from victory. Someone yelled, "Strike the bum out!", one of the more pleasant aspersions Bailey could hear.

"Listen to that crowd," Steve Drake said.

"Oh, hell," said Keough, "that ain't nothin'. You ever been to Yankee Stadium?"

Yes, I have, Bailey answered silently. He didn't know if Keough ever had. Bailey had had the fortune to be umpiring the final series one season when Boston and New York faced off in three games that would decide the division winner. Three games with crowds that dwarfed what was here today, which was a decent crowd for a dying league. Hell I think they had more peanut vendors in Yankee Stadium than they've got fans here today. Don't remember who won, but it was a thrill.

"Let's go," said Bailey.

Smaller crowd, less famous league, but an important game in its own right, and even Bailey began to feel the tension. Now is not when you want to blow a call. To the people here, *this* is far more important than what might be taking place in Yankee Stadium.

With the loudest noise of the day in the background Sevan's pitch came in, a good pitch, a tempting pitch for the batter, who only managed to nick the ball and send it spinning in the dirt.

"Dammit!" Dakota Keough cursed.

The noise eased of for a few seconds, than rose up again as the crowd waited for the pitcher and batter to get ready to duel again. Again Sevan took his time. For a moment he covered his face with his glove and Bailey thought he was laughing. Keough called time and stepped out, assuming Bailey had allowed it.

The umpire didn't say anything; the batter is suppose to get my permission but now's not the time to push the issue. He waited patiently for Keough to get back in the batter's box, than pointed at Sevan to say, you're on. Sevan looked intent, glanced at first, and flipped the ball to the first baseman, an easy lob meant to either bug the batter, or because he was not quite ready to throw the next pitch.

It didn't bother Bailey a bit. He never let himself think about what he had to do after the game was over, so he didn't worry about how long it took. He tried to keep the pace moving, liked a steady pace, but any good umpire knew when to let the players alone. Now was the time. If Sevan wanted to dawdle, let him; if Keough wanted to take time out and fuss with the bat and rub dirt in his hands, let him.

The buzz began again and twenty thousand and some odd number of people rose up yelling and whistling and clapping their hands. The base runners edged away from safety, Bailey crouched, his left hand just touching the top of the catcher's shoulder. Sevan waited patiently for Keough to get in the box, and when the batter was set, he stretched and threw.

THE CLOSER

JOHN ZANTO yawned in his seat in the bullpen behind the centerfield fence, far enough away from home plate that even Al Lucky rarely sent a ball there. Trouble with being this far away is that it was difficult to see what was going on. Which is why the inhabitants of the bullpen often watched the game on TV.

Zanto, whose nickname was 'Junkyard', because of the assortment of rare and unusual pitches in his repertoire, stood up and walked to the water cooler.

"Anything?" he said.

The bullpen coach, Joe Walker shook his head. "Nah."

Just the same Walker looked at Phil Hood, usually a starter, but who was in the pen today in case a fastballing lefty was needed to get an out or two, and nodded.

Zanto, or Junkyard, not being one who threw very hard, didn't need much time to warm up. It's not like you can practice your knuckleball too much, because no matter how much you did, neither you, the pitcher, nor anyone else, could predict with any accuracy how much the ball would break. However, for reasons that defy analysis, the batter coming up now, Dakota Keough, had shown an uncanny knack for handling Junkyard's knuckler, so it wasn't likely that the call would come yet.

The next batter, however, a lefthander, might go to Hood, and Walker knew that without needing to be called by the manager, Frank Jensen. The pre-game coaches' meeting had discussed this exact situation, and if it looked like it would occur, Hood needed to be ready.

Junkyard, on the other hand, would come in only if Sevan was in serious trouble and the game was close. And then it might take the entire coaching staff and a couple players to drag Sevan off the mound. Everybody knew that Sevan liked to complete his games, but he was realistic about using the bullpen when he knew he had lost his best stuff, his speed, or control. As this game would decide the divisional championship Sevan was going to be more inclined to want to finish, so with a 2-0 lead going into the ninth inning, the bullpen was not yet very active.

So sure enough, at that moment the bullpen phone rang. Without waiting to be told anything Johnny picked up his glove. Rick Taylor, a backup catcher, grabbed his mitt and took his place behind the bullpen plate, ready to help Johnny warm up. The closer threw easily at first, a few knucklers, some of which Taylor was able to catch, while next to him Phil Hood was throwing nothing but serious fastballs. If Hood got the call he was going to give it all he had, his hardest stuff, and go for the strikeout.

Once it became certain that the Continental League would be disbanded, there were numerous bullshit sessions where players reminisced about their careers, about great games and crazy games, wild plays and strange characters. The bullpen was a great place for sitting around and getting nostalgic about the 'good old days.'

Just the other day the bullpen denizens were talking about the longest game in Continental League history, the 23-inning affair between the Jets and the Texans.

"I think it was 22 innings," said Joe Walker.

"No, 23; I remember because I was in there at the end," said Johnny.

"Well, I remember you were in there, but I don't remember what inning it was."

"Yes, sir, it was 23. I remember because of the strike outs."

"How so?"

"We went 18 or 19 innings, it was four o'clock in the morning, everybody was tired, the umps were bleary-eyed, so they called it for the night."

"Why, if the game was still tied?"

"Because it was four o'clock in the morning, dodo! Both teams were off the next day so it was decided we'd pick up the game in the afternoon. Wasn't much of a crowd since few people knew about it."

The thing about baseball is, a game could, in theory, never end. Some people think that's awful, but then they aren't baseball fans. A football game, a basketball game, a hockey game, they are controlled by a clock, moving inevitably to a defined finish. A football team down by four touchdowns with five minutes to go in the game, is not going to win. A baseball team down by four runs going into the ninth inning is not *likely* to win, but they *might*, and it's been done. There is always hope, and remember what Yogi said.

For a baseball fan there isn't anything much more satisfying than to be sitting in one's favorite chair, late on a weekend night, watching two teams go at it inning after inning, while managers juggle their rosters.

And unlike the other major sports, once a player is out of a game, he can't return, no matter how many innings it takes. So when a manager replaces a power hitter who runs like he's pulling a plow, for

86

a pinch runner, he has to be sure he won't need that power hitter again. And when he brings in his ace relief pitcher he has to consider that if the game goes on and on, the ace won't be available at a more crucial moment.

Most games do get completed in nine innings and that's the way the players and managers figure it for the most part. There have been some spectacular exceptions. In the National League there was a game once that went 26 innings. In the American League a game went 25 innings and took more than eight hours spread over two days to complete.

"The crazy thing," Johnny said, "was that the Texans had used up everybody except the three pitchers geared to start their next series. We'd used up everybody except our top starters and me. So we put in Al's brother, Don; remember him, the infielder?"

A few nods, even from those who didn't remember him.

"Almost as a joke, the Texans brought in Frank's brother, Ed."

"Oh, yeah, the guy they called 'Boots'," said Walker.'

"Well, that was unfortunate for him, because he was a decent player."

"Why'd they call him 'Boots'?" asked Wayner, one of the long relievers.

"Poor guy made errors on two consecutive plays in the seventh game to give us the title; think it was back in season 26. The guy was a good fielder otherwise, but that's how it goes sometimes. The name stuck with him."

"So what about the long game?"

"Yeah, well both teams had their third string catchers in, and if anybody had gotten hurt I think that team would've had to play short a man, if that's allowed; I don't know if it is. Anyway, Boots and Don Lucky go out there and Don gives up a homer and the Texans take the lead. Boots almost wins the game, but with two outs Knoll hits an inside the park homer, can you believe. Play at the plate almost took out the catcher and the umpire, but the ball rolled free and the game was tied again.

"Actually they pitched fairly well, for infielders. Of course the hitters were still tired. Guys were falling asleep in the dugout. So no one scores for the next three or four innings, whatever it was. Boots is tired of pitching, so is Don, but we still had me. Like I'd been forgotten.

"Don walked the first two batters in the 23rd, so I came in. 'It's about time!' I said. I manage to get out of the inning. Got a strike out, then Kenny made a real nice catch in center, and then I got the last out on another strike out, and it was the 23rd strike out for our pitchers, that's how I remember, one per inning."

Johnny stopped talking, his story apparently over.

"So what happened then?" one of the younger players asked, one who hadn't been in the league long enough to know about the long game.

"Oh, yeah", Johnny said. "Knoll beat out a bunt for a hit, and after I screwed up two sacrifice bunt attempts, I swung away and tripled to win the game. Only triple I ever got. So I remember it well."

When Harlem Joe Havey walked a nervous chatter began to rise from the crowd. When the next batter, Ben Train, singled, there was a stirring, a hum, the opening of sleepy eyes in the bullpen.

Johnny, *the* Junkyard, had saved umpteen games for the Jets, including a bunch for Sevan. He would love to save this one but didn't care much as long as the Jets won. He knew he'd have a chance for a save or two in the Championship Series. What he didn't want was to be sitting on his ass collecting splinters while Jack blew the game because he was too stubborn to come out. It'll be up to Frank.

"What's the count," a voice from the bench said.

"One and one, ain't you watching the game?" said another voice.

"Nah, I'm sleeping. Wake me when it's over."

"Don't count your playoff money yet, Cowboys got two on and Dak's coming to bat."

How to pitch on various counts was a constant topic of conversation among pitchers. The general consensus was that in recent years the hitters have been helping the pitchers by taking too many first pitches. It was a theme they didn't care to share with the hitters, even their fellow teammates.

"Part of it is the manager's fault," claimed Joe Walker. "They don't let guys swing on 2-0, even 3-1, and we know that (we, meaning the fraternity of pitchers), so it makes it safer for us to groove one to get a certain strike."

"Yeah," agreed Johnny. "I've noticed that more over the years. They're always thinking they'll get something better to hit later. But if I've got my control, the best pitch they'll get to hit is the first one, because I want to get a strike ahead of them."

"What if they're sittin' on it, Johnny?"

Johnny shrugged. "That's the risk. All I'm saying is that more and more they're letting the first one go by. On the first pitch I may take extra care to make sure I put it where the ump has no doubt it's in the zone. A smart hitter might crush it," he added, with a grin.

"So you're saying the hitters are getting dumber, hey?"

"I think they're more worried about the stats. You get a walk, it helps your damn on-base percentage, and doesn't hurt the batting average. But me, if I was managing, I want my RBI guys to think run production, not on-base percentage."

"They're trying to tire us out, make us throw more pitches."

"Hmmph."

"Does Frank manage like all the others, you think?" asked one of the young pitchers, a long reliever who usually worked non-vital situations.

"Not as much, because he was a hitter, and a good one, so he knows how hard it is to hit. When he's got men on base and his 3, 4, 5 hitters up, he wants them to drive the runners home, not go to bat thinking about working a walk. It depends on the situation. Top of the inning, get on anyway you can; man on third, two out, you gonna work a walk and leave the job to the next guy?

"Now, I've never talked to him about this, it's just an observation. But that's how I'd manage. Same with the three-oh. Everybody takes it and we know they will, so we put a cookie right there, strike one, good for us."

"So how come Sevan likes to start off some hitters by throwing way inside?" asked the young middle reliever.

Johnny looked at the kid, smiled and said, "You win three hundred games, kid, you can throw anyway you want."

"Pickoff play at second," a voice said.

A moment later the prediction came true as Sevan wheeled and tried to nail the runner, Havey, off second base. It was close and elicited several moans from the bullpen.

"Thought we had him! Damn!"

Johnny didn't look; too far away to tell how close a call it was anyway.

When John Zanto began his baseball career he was a starting pitcher with a good fastball and a wicked curve. But he hurt his arm and when he recovered he could never again attain the speed necessary to fly one by a professional hitter on a consistent basis. He got bombed for far too many home runs. So he began to experiment with unusual and off speed pitches, especially the knuckleball. Some pitchers can never learn to throw one, and most don't need to, as long as they have the usual assortment. He also learned to throw a screwball, which was almost as rare as the knuckler.

But what drove the hitters crazy was Johnny's change of pace. No matter how often they saw it, the pitch was nearly impossible to time.

Mike Williams had famously said, "That piece of junk comes in there so slow, I swung three times before it got to the plate. Struck out on one pitch. He throws junk, but it's great junk'."

The comment led to the nickname, 'Junkyard'. Now well over 40 years old, the Junkyard (the addition of *the* to the sobriquet Junkyard was sometimes used by admirers as an added note of appreciation for the closer's skills) had no intention of retiring. But at his age he didn't expect either of the other major leagues to show an interest. He'd have to find something to do with his time. Surely there are pitchers who have lost a few miles per hour off their fastball who'd be eager to learn what I can teach them, he suggested whenever the talk in the bullpen turned to 'what are you going to do when the league ends?'

Johnny caught Walker's eyes and he nodded. The coach picked up the phone and was connected to the dugout, to pitching coach Jim Roberts.

"Any time you want him." A pause as he listened, then, "Yeah, I don't doubt it." Walker laughed as he hung up the phone.

"Jim says you're in if Dak gets on, but you may have to help drag Jack off the mound."

Johnny smiled and went back to throwing knucklers to his catcher. The ball dipped and rolled away. "It's good today, Junk," said Rich Taylor.

"Humph," was Johnny's reply. He knew better than anyone that the knuckler could be moving like a drunk bumblebee in the bullpen, but five minutes later, with the game on the line, it might come in straight as a Robin Hood arrow.

People in the stands were stamping feet, whistling, and clapping their hands. Everyone in the bullpen could hear the crowd noise rev up. They were all wide-awake now, standing near the fence and watching, or at the television set, where you could actually see better.

Johnny stopped throwing and asked, "Full count?"

"Yeah, of course. I think Sevan did it on purpose to build up the suspense."

"I would not be surprised," someone said.

Ohs and ahs filled the stadium and the buzz decreased after the batter swung at the 3-2 offering and pounded it into the ground. But the lowered noise level lasted only a few seconds before it picked up again.

"Throw to first, Jack," one of the relievers said.

Johnny was watching intently but asked Walker, "You sure Frank wants me, not Phil, against Arnett?"

The scheduled batter after Keough was one of the Arnett boys, the son of one of the early stars of the league. He was a free-swinging lefty and Phil Hood was exceptionally affective against left-handed hitters.

"That's what he said; he could change his mind. How have you done against him."

"Fine. Hey, if the knuckler's working, I'm pretty sure I can take him. If not, well, if I get a second chance the screwgie might entice him to beat one into the dirt."

"Okay, if he asks me, you're good to go, right?"

"Affirmative," Johnny said.

The crowd had to reset its cheering and stomping as Sevan tossed to first base, Keough stepped out of the batter's box, and everyone waited for the show to resume.

"If he gets Dak out, then what?" Johnny asked.

Joe Walker shook his head. "Dunno. We'll find out real soon."

Everybody in the bullpen stopped whatever they were doing and watched as Jack Sevan reared back and fired the full count pitch.

THE FINAL PITCH

JACK SEVAN stretched and threw the full count pitch. Normally in this particular situation, this count, this batter, this sequence, this exact moment in the game, Sevan would have thrown a fastball, probably the cutter. And being the stubborn ace that he was, his choice of pitches would trump Drake's, if they disagreed. But this time, when the catcher signaled a change in tactic, Sevan nodded immediately. He knew he was tired and his fastball didn't have as much on it as it did earlier in the game. A mile or two per hour slower or a quarter of an inch less movement could make the difference between a pop up or a home run with a good hitter.

Dakota Keough still had excellent eye sight, even at the advanced age of thirty-nine. No baseball player could expect to hit a round ball with a round bat, squarely, when it's moving at between eighty and a hundred miles per hour, and moves like a Mexican jumping bean, without near-perfect vision.

So while he was expecting Sevan's best fast ball, as the ball began to leave the pitcher's hand Keough thought he had a glimpse of the grip, one that suggested not a fastball, but Sevan's famous Marilyn Monroe curve ball. The one that seemed to curl around the bat and made the crowd ooh in appreciation as the helpless batter flailed away.

A curveball has topspin, not backspin, like a fastball, and this creates a high-pressure zone on top of the ball, which deflects the ball and causes it to move downward in its flight. It is thrown slower than a fastball but the trajectory can fool the hitter into thinking it will be outside the strike zone, then curve in, fooling the batter who stands there with the bat on his shoulder while the umpire calls him out. Or, it may look like a beautiful pitch to hit, then curve outside the strike zone and leave the batter swinging helplessly at empty air.

Of course there was not enough time to think about this, or dwell on his options. It was just a split-second observation that kicked up a residue of a memory of something Keough might or might not have experienced on one of those all too rare occasions when he guessed correctly on a pitch, and realized it wasn't a merely a lucky guess.

Expecting a fastball the batter would likely swing too soon, and miss the curve ball before it even got to the plate. If he did time it correctly the ball would fall off the table, as the saying went, dipping down below his knees. But it would cross the heart of the plate, and no umpire on the face of the earth could say for certain whether the ball came in a quarter of an inch above or below the knee. Strike three, go sit down.

Of course the worse fear of the pitcher was that the curve ball would 'hang', that is, its downward path would not occur soon enough and as it reached the plate it would appear to the batter to just sit there for a moment, a mere flicker of a wink, a micro-second too short to measure, but to the batter it would be as if the ball had been set up on a tee, like for five year olds. He could kill it.

Another breaking pitch, thrown by only a few pitchers, usually lefthanders, is the screwball. When thrown by a southpaw, a screwball breaks from right to left, moving down and in on a left-handed batter and down and away from a batter on the right side. In other words, generally opposite of what a curveball does.

Maybe it got its name because southpaws are the ones who usually employ the pitch, and us southpaws are considered to have a few screws loose, Jack Sevan thought as he released the ball.

Many times it made no difference, but a big league hitter can do different things with a fastball as opposed to a breaking ball. How the defense sets up for a particular pitch may decide whether the hitter gets on base, or is put out because the fielder positioned himself according to the pitch. In this case it mattered because Keough was so fooled he almost came out the better for it.

If he had time to vocalize what was happening, Keough would have said: Too late, dammit, it's his screwball, not the curve...sucker is gonna break away from me...I can't let it go by...it looks good, but moving away...

The batter grimaced as he extended his arms, desperate to make contact with a pitch that was going to be farther away than he preferred, but probably on the black edge of the plate. Keough wouldn't be able to get all his power behind such a swing so there was no way he could drive the ball deep to the outfield, which was not necessary in this situation. A dying quail, or a wounded duck arcing to right center would be wonderful for the Cowboys if the ball didn't hang up long enough for Phillips or Lucky to get to it.

Drake held his mitt where he expected the ball to be, if Keough didn't get a piece of it. Sevan's screwgie broke away beautifully and Drake knew Keough was fooled. Sevan, on the mound, completing his follow through, also knew it was good pitch, a strike out maybe, or a lovely three-bouncer to Brick who'd start a game ending double play. Piece of cake.

But Keough didn't miss completely. He didn't make a real solid connection, not with much power, striking the ball with top inch of the bat. Keough felt a clunking sound that indicated it wasn't solid contact, but he was strong enough to punch the ball out of the infield, a low line drive that the second baseman thought he could reach. But it wasn't that low and it arced out towards right-centerfield.

Damn, thought Brick, that sucker might drop in. On second base stood Havey, who had retreated when at first it looked like Brick would catch the ball on the fly. Now, as he saw the ball flare towards the outfield he judged that neither the speedy centerfielder, Ken Phillips, nor Al Lucky who had moved a few steps more towards center just before the pitch, were going to be able to nab the ball in the air. Havey made his decision and darted for third, his eyes searching for the third base coach. The coach was watching the ball and the outfielders; in an instant he would have to gauge whether to send Havey home or hold him at third.

Drake flipped off his mask and made several calculations in the time it took for the ball to pass over Brick's futile leap. If Kenny or Al can catch up to it, we'll double off Havey, end of game, sweet victory. If not, we may have a play here, or a cutoff to keep Train from reaching third.

Sevan was running from the mound to take a position in back of Drake to cover in case of an overthrow. We don't want two runs scoring here. Goddamn, I thought I'd fooled him, sombitch.

Sandusky moved at an angle towards the mound, aligning himself with home plate, preparing for a throw from Lucky. He would have to decide whether to let the throw go through, risking the runners moving to second and third, and hope it would nab Havey at home. He glanced at third and saw Havey on his way there, the coach undecided yet on what signal to give his base runner.

In centerfield Ken Phillips, a veteran ball hawk, knew he had no chance. He'd been playing Keough deep to avoid having the slugger belt one over his head, and there was no possibility he could catch this on the fly. If he went for it on the bounce, he'd be coming in on the ball while moving towards the right field foul line, and would have to re-position his body for the throw. Al, coming in from his position, would have a better angle.

Too late to yell, Phillips realized Lucky was going to dive for the ball. If it got past him the ball could roll to the fence and score both runners, maybe allow Keough to make it all the way to third base. He instantly adjusted his approach to back up Lucky.

Al Lucky was a quick judge and seemed to begin his move before the ball had met the bat. It was the way Keough's body had moved that told Lucky the ball, if Keough hit it all, was going to dart towards his right. Lucky began moving and saw the liner clear Brick's glove and began its descent. He thought he could reach it and was sure he'd have a chance to double Havey off second.

A few years ago the runner on second wouldn't have budged, knowing Lucky would more than likely catch the ball, even if he had to roll over a few times while doing it. Lucky knew that, too, but it wasn't a few years ago, it was now, today, and the outfielder felt like he was moving in slow motion as the ball was dropping much too rapidly.

Lucky didn't have to think about the risk of letting the ball roll past him; he trusted Phillips to back him up. There had been a few misadventures over the years where Lucky was confident he could

98

catch a sinking line drive with a dive to the earth, but had missed, resulting in a triple or even an inside-the-park home run. But far more often than not he made the play, or at least got to the ball on a short hop. This time it was going to be close.

Lucky dove for the ball, stretching his body to the limit, parallel to the ground, oblivious to the risk of injury and saw the white flash is it hit the green grass an inch from his glove. He saw and felt it hop into his glove and felt it securely in the webbing as he rolled over and bounced up in one motion.

The scene on the field was exactly as he'd seen it in his mind's eye while he was chasing the fly ball. Havey was rounding third base, the coach signaling him with a wild pin wheeling motion of his arm. Ben Train, the runner from first, had moved halfway to second and as he saw the ball hit grass before it hit leather, had begun his dash to second. Sandusky was lined up for a throw but from this distance Lucky knew he didn't need a cut off man.

Drake was stationed like the Colossus of Rhodes in front of home plate. Lucky pulled the ball out of the glove as he was completing his bounce and in one clean motion whipped it towards home. He felt a burning sensation as if a hot knife had been stuck into his arm, right at the elbow. The pain shocked him and his face showed it, a look that would grace the front cover of Sports Illustrated next week. But the ball had already left his hand, a laser to the catcher.

Sandusky instantly knew the throw was on target, maybe perfect. Drake saw the ball leave Lucky's hand and glanced up the line to note Havey's progress; it was going to be tight. Old man Harlem Joe was chugging his way home, a freight train carrying its precious cargo of one run, a tired and powerful engine on its last mission. The catcher braced himself.

As Ben Train hit second base he could see that Lucky was going home with the throw. He couldn't worry about what happened to Havey, his job was to get to third base, and maybe Keough could reach second, though he wasn't exactly Speedy Gonzalez.

The batter, Keough, now a base runner, rounded first and slowed, waiting to see what Train was going to do, and whether Sandusky was going to cut off the throw. With a two run lead he could do that, concede the run, and try to either get Train going to third, or get Keough if he strayed too far between first and second base.

Even Sevan, watching from behind Drake, estimated that conceding Havey's run might be a good choice if the Jets got one of the other runners out. But Lucky's throw looked so good it'd be a shame to waste it. That was what Sandusky decided, too.

The collision at home plate sent Drake and Havey flying backwards in a cloud of dust. Bailey, the umpire, got knocked over, too. The throw had clearly beaten Havey and Drake had clearly caught it a split second before Havey crashed into him. Drake had had just enough time to cover his treasure with his bare hand as he bent to tag Havey. The only question was did Drake hang on to the ball.

Three bodies lay as one big bundle, several feet away from the plate. Drake held up his glove with the ball stuck firmly in the pocket for all to see. Jughead Bailey rose to his knees and gave a firm 'Out!' signal, his throat too full of dust to give a verbal call.

Still holding his glove in the air, Drake fell back, his legs and arms spread out as if he'd been shot dead. Keough stumbled trying to get up and fell on Drake's legs, pining him to the ground. As Drake's left arm fell to the ground the glove hit, raising dust, and freeing the ball, which dribbled away in the general direction of the first base dugout.

Coming into third base Ben Train watched the action at home and saw the ball roll away. He wasn't sure what the call at home had been. He hadn't seen Bailey's signal and with the crowd noise he wouldn't have heard a call even if Bailey had yelled at the top of his lungs. Since it was a Jets' crowd the exuberant thundering of cheers indicated Havey had been out.

Maybe it was a burst of enthusiasm, or simply a case of a player seeing an opportunity. But Train hadn't grasped the whole picture. He didn't see Sevan standing in back of the clump of players laying on the ground, else he wouldn't have taken the chance. All he saw was the ball rolling away and at the moment he saw it, no one was going for the ball. Later he said he thought it was the batboy standing behind the pile of dazed players and umpire.

True, there was a moment, as caught on video, where everybody seemed to stop, as if frozen in their tracks, as if posing for a picture of that exact wink in time. Then Ben Train, barely slowing as he rounded third base, broke the reverie with his mad charge to home plate.

They would talk about this moment in years to come, like stories they used to tell during the days of the 'hot stove league.' Stories they would have told in the first days of spring training, when the players were stretching easily, tossing soft lobs, slowing getting back in gear for another season. With no more spring trainings or off-season meetings, no batting practice bull sessions, stories of the great days of the Continental League would have to be told at reunions, big and small, sometimes the annual league reunion, sometimes a team reunion, often just a bunch of guys who had played together but now gathered to burn a steak and share tales of glory.

And all the tales were of glory, never sadness. The sadness was only in that there were no more days of glory, for win or lose, those were days of glory, every one of them.

Sevan picked up the ball and looked out onto the diamond to see if there was a pending play. He expected Train to be on third, and wasn't sure about Keough. He looked at Keough and saw him only a few feet from first base; he'd decided not to risk trying for second. But then Sevan saw Keough look towards third and as he did he, the Cowboy star began to run to second. Sevan was startled and was about to throw the ball to second base when a shout caught his attention. He looked to his left and saw Ben Train, emulating his name, barreling down the third base line. Sevan was surprised again and wondered what the heck is he doing. Then he grasped the surprise move by Train and with Drake still flat on his back, unable to take a throw from Sevan, the pitcher charged to meet the onrushing Cowboy. The runner slid, spikes first, and Sevan dived across home plate, holding the ball out in front of him as he did so. With the ball in his left hand he tagged the sliding foot of Ben Train.

Jughead Bailey croaked, "Out!", then louder, he repeated, "Yer Out!"

Two of Seven's fingers were broken on the play and he was never able to throw the screwball again, and his curve wasn't too nifty either. But he never threw much anymore except to play catch with his kids.

*

"The Prey"

For not the first time Andrew Jones wondered whether there was an easier way to make a million dollars, like something that didn't involve dying. Sure, it wasn't guaranteed that he'd have to die, but the deck was stacked, the odds were against him, his goose was cooked, and so forth.

Maybe he deserved to die. After all, he'd gotten a break when the D.A. accepted his plea bargain to second-degree murder. They hadn't felt they had a strong enough case to get him on a first-degree charge, lucky break, since I'd been thinking of killing that bastard Harry Owens for months, Andy recalled. So I get eight to ten, time off for good behavior; Ha! Of course I behaved, wasn't much else to do.

It was those damn parole regulations that got to me. Having to report all the time, can't leave the state, no going to my old hangouts, no gambling; Damn! What's a guy to do for fun?

His head itched. Andy tried to scratch it but the helmet he was required to wear made scratching impossible. He was sweaty, itchy, the helmet was too tight, and he was getting hungry. The helmet was like one of those miner's hats, except besides a light it had a camera, one that brought to the viewers everything Andy saw. All those voyeurs sitting at home, waiting to see how I get it-- creeps! I'll show them, somehow, I don't know, but somehow I'll win this damn hunt and then I'll have the last laugh.

His arm itched, too, where they had placed the 'device', as it was affectionately called. This wonderful piece of new age technology was a combination GPS and electrode. It traced Andy's movements so that even if he was deep in the brush and the cameras couldn't show enough to identify his location, the computers always knew his position and revealed it to the audience on computer-generated maps. Persons on the Internet could track Andy's movements, and see where he was in relation to anything else on the island, including the Hunter. But neither the Hunter nor the Prey had access to that information. The device also monitored Andy's vital signs; RealDrama didn't want Andy to get sick before he could be killed.

It had long ago dawned on Andy he couldn't go home even if he survived, not without getting arrested for violating his parole. I wonder what they'd give me this time? Maybe it'd be worth it, what with a million bucks in the bank. Something to think about later.

He was started by a sound, like the crack of a branch, a sound that jarred him out of his reverie and caused his heart to palpitate.

He thought he'd been ready to die—for a million bucks, which would go to his wife and his twelve-year-old son. That was the deal. He agreed to be hunted, on live television, not to mention big screen theaters, the Internet, and sports bars all over the country and the world. His designated heirs would receive the money, which was in escrow, as long as he didn't violate any of the rules.

The rules were few: he couldn't kill himself, he couldn't take off his video helmet, and he couldn't purposely damage any of the many cameras that covered virtually every square inch of the two-square mile island. Other than that he was on his own, just he in his cargo pants style shorts, dark green tee-shirt that did give him a modicum of camouflage, a good pair of hiking boots, and the knife, his only weapon. Andy also had a backpack strapped on which contained several bottles of water and energy bars. The pack was already getting heavy but Andy knew he needed to lug the water with him, at least until he found a source of fresh water, which he was told did exist on the island.

Andy didn't know exactly where the island was located, other than that he'd been told it was near the equator, at least five hundred miles from any other piece of land, and that is was a fairly new island, as geographical ages go. Far off the shipping and air routes, no country had claimed the island, so RealDrama, Inc. had claimed it, move in a crew and built facilities, and guarded it with two aging destroyers it had purchased from a militaristic South East Asian nation to be unnamed, and numerous machine-gun ready guards who roamed the perimeter of the island.

Protests from many nations, including the United States, marches in the streets of hundreds of cities, and referendums in the United Nations had not deterred RealDrama, Inc. They owned the island, they could set their own laws, and lots of people wanted to see gladiators fight to the death, old-West style gunfights, sword fights that spilled blood, not those pansy-ass Olympic fencing matches, and now this, a hunt to the death.

It wasn't meant to be a fair fight. Those might come later, but RealDrama wanted to pit a desperate man facing impossible odds, to get viewers rooting for him as he scrambled for his life, knowing the payoff was immense. The million bucks was Andy's payoff, but he didn't expect to collect. He knew he'd been the proto-typical jackass all his life, and this was his last ditch effort to do something for the wife and son he loved but didn't know how to take care of.

The Hunter, unnamed to Andy, was also guaranteed a million dollars, a small investment for RealDrama, considering viewers were paying $99.95 to receive the telecast. Andy did a quick calculation: if only a million homes, or bars, theatres, whatever, purchased the show, RealDrama would gross a hundred million dollars, before expenses! Damn, I should have held out for a lot more than a million dollars. Bastards are gonna get rich on my death.

Andy heard another crack and stood dead still. He turned his head one way then the other, his eyes straining to see through the dense foliage. In every direction it was green. He no longer heard the hum of insects.

The Hunter couldn't have caught up with him already, could he, Andy wondered. Andy had been told he'd be given a one-hour head start before the Hunter could begin to seek the Prey, that being Andy. Without a watch Andy could not tell how long it'd been since he'd set out from the command post, waving like a fool to the dozens of cameras and news reporters. He'd even been able to sell his autograph, at a hundred bucks a crack.

Then he heard a rushing in the trees above him and Andy ducked down on the ground, more scared than he'd ever been, even the time that lunatic in the prison came at him with the crude shiv he'd manufactured from a bedspring.

The chatter from the trees terrified Andy for a second, and he was relieved when he saw the monkey, one of the residents of this island jungle. Andy stood and wiped the sweat off his forehead with his left arm. His right hand ached and he looked down to see that he held the knife in a death grip. He hadn't remembered taking it out of its pouch but had done so automatically when he'd heard the first sound. He eased his grip and took a deep breath.

Then Andy saw the camera, bolted to the tree right next to the monkey, who was reaching for the odd device, odd, that is, to be in the monkey's tree. Andy knew, at least he been informed, that there were cameras all over the island, so that virtually nothing the hunter and the hunted could do wouldn't be covered. He only hoped they'd have the good sense to shut the damn thing off when he needed to relieve himself.

Suddenly the monkey screamed as a charge shot out from the screen that surrounded the camera. Hmm, laughed Andy, an electrical charge. He watched the monkey leap high up into the tree and then swing on a vine into the next tree.

A dull plunk reverberated and next to his head a chunk of tree bark was sliced off as if chopped with a machete. Andy dropped to the ground instantly. High above him the shrieks of hundreds of birds pierced the air, birds the hunted man hadn't realized were there.

Andy hugged the ground, unsure whether he should lay still or rise up and run. The damp earth smelled of decaying vegetation, the air around him, of sweet, perfumed flowers. When Andy opened his eyes a bug stared at him, a centipede or something equally ugly, as long as his middle finger. He blew on the bug and diverted it from its path that was leading to Andy's nose. He felt dampness and thought he had peed his pants, but it was simply the wet of the dirt seeping into his clothes.

Damn, now I'll be wet and clammy the rest of...what, the rest of my life? Andy listened hard; there was no sound. Then, the first resurgence of bird sounds, a distance away now. He dared to raise his head and look around him. He could see little but foliage, the thick, green growth of the lush jungle. In front of him knee high plants of incredible variety surrounded him. Rising upward were banana and coconut trees, which would provide him food, he'd been advised,

108

should he live long enough to need it, bougainvillea, bamboo, and a variety of trees from which hung long vines. He half expected, half hoped, that Tarzan would come flying through the canopy to save him.

Maybe it was just a wild shot; maybe the Hunter was trying to get a reaction, maybe get a scream out of me. Slowly Andy rose to one knee and again scanned his environment, struggling to see through the flora for a hint of another human being. He heard a faint click and turned quickly in the direction. Above him, another camera eyed him, the click having been the slight motion as it adjusted its point of view.

Damn! The whole world is laughing at me, seeing me crawling in the mud, shivering and scared. Screw this; if I'm going to die I'll at least make a good show of it. With that thought Andy rose up and began to schlep his way forward, lashing at plants and vines that tore at his face, which was nearly every other step. He couldn't move fast without making noise, so if the Hunter was nearby he'd find Andy by sight or sound. So it was either move his ass or stay still and get bitten to death by hoards of humongous insects. He felt a bite on his arm and scratched at it, then yelped when he saw some kind of bug as big as a silver dollar setting there, enjoining a snack of Andy's skin. He scraped it off with his knife, and then examined the rest of his body.

His arms and legs were covered with dirt, bits of vegetation, and crawly things, some dead, some alive. His clothes were wet and dirty. He scraped at the bugs, again pondering that all over the world people were watching him, laughing at him, maybe a few rooting for him. Was Hattie watching, with Kerry, their son? Did they care if he lived or died, or were they just waiting for the million dollars?

When this adventure began Andy didn't care a whole lot about living any more. When he'd heard about the plan to televise live human hunts he thought that might be something to see. When RealDrama announced they were offering a million dollars, to both the hunter and the prey, the company was overwhelmed with bids, mostly to be the Hunter. Hundreds of deer hunters thought they were qualified to go after a human being, and would have no compunctions about killing the person.

The idea was that the prey would be someone who was on death row. But the plan ran into all kinds of legal issues, not to mention moral and religious issues. Seeing as how more and more communities were allowing persons to carry handguns, the popularity of violent barehanded and kickboxing events and various forms of 'cage fighting,' RealDrama hadn't anticipated such protests.

Soon they were barred from advertising their events on TV or in print, but who cared with Internet available to nearly everybody. The only bit of information that RealDrama was exceptionally careful about revealing was the exact location of the island. The United States Government had determined where the island was, and had shared that information with other governments, but the politicians were stymied. The island was truly located in international waters and did not show up on any charts that anyone could locate. It was as if the island had appeared out of nowhere.

And in fact, that's about what had happened. Geologists explained it was possible, and in fact, not extremely rare, for bits of land to pop up in the ocean. After all, island building was going on all the time. Usually the process is well know in advance by geologists, such as the new Hawaiian island that was growing up from the sea floor and in about 10,000 years would become an addition to the vacation paradise.

Unexpected outgrowths were generally small chunks of land, not more than a few acres, and usually collapsed on themselves back into the sea within months. In those cases in recent history where an island continued to grow and become a viable space of land, it occurred near land already within the claimed territory of a nation, and there was no argument about which country had a right to claim it.

In this case the new island had appeared without warning, albeit in an isolated part of the ocean that no one cared about, and it had grown faster and to a larger size than geologists expected. Still, they urged caution, insisting that the island was unstable and could be washed away with little warning. Anyone going there, they warned, was taking a major risk with their lives.

This only served to make RealDrama's plans more exciting. The executives intended to milk the public for all they could get, as quickly as they could, and keep their fingers crossed that they received adequate warning if the island began to sink.

Without being able to use men on death row RealDrama looked elsewhere. They received many more volunteers than they expected and had to carefully eliminate the weird, the crazy, the ones with a death wish, the ones they gauged would not make "good television." They wanted someone who wasn't afraid to die, but who had people they cared about and were willing to die for to see that their loved ones were financially secure.

At first RealDrama wanted only single men, to cut down the chances of lawsuits by family survivors. But eventually they decided that a man willing to put his life on the line for his family's financial wellbeing would garner a lot of public empathy. Finally the list was cut down to men (no women, not this first time, to hell with that nonsense) who were married with at least one child, but were estranged, were not able to provide financially, appeared to have some basic outdoors skills, and despite their problems with the law (and nearly all of these men had had serious problems with the law), could accept dying, but would make a serious effort at trying to defeat the Hunter, who would be far better armed and equipped than the Prey. RealDrama also wasn't concerned that for a man like Andy he'd be breaking parole; that was his problem should he survive, nobody's if he died, which they expected.

As for the Hunter, this was even more difficult. RealDrama wanted someone who was an excellent outdoorsman and hunter, but not someone who was well known to the public, lest the public turn against RealDrama in the unlikely scenario that the Hunter lost the contest. They didn't want some famous actor who saw himself as the great white hunter getting himself killed in front of millions of people. Besides, no famous, rich person needed a mere million dollars.

In this case they decided to choose from unmarried persons, figuring that would grab an audience of young women eager to cheer for this daring young man, and possibly set the stage for recurring episodes. The winner was drawn from a random selection of the final hundred candidates, but his name was not yet released to the public, and he was forbidden by contract from revealing his identity until after the show.

Andy continued to hack at the brush, trying to clear a path. To where, he didn't know. He had no map of the island, except in his head. He'd been shown a plot map of the island for a few minutes to give him an idea of the general geography and contour of his new world. The map had marked where fresh water was and also the places he could not go, that is, the fenced area where RealDrama was headquartered-where the computers were, where the crew ate and slept, where there was fresh food and comfortable beds. But don't even think about it, Andy was advised. The fence is electrified and even if you did get into the compound, that would also nullify your contract and you'd lose your million dollars. He'd been allowed five minutes to study the map, and he assumed, so had the Hunter.

Based on the sun's location, which he could barely see through the thick growth above him, vines and an assortment of exotic plants that grew so fast you could almost see it happening, and his recollection of the map, he should be heading east, towards a steep cliff. At the bottom of the cliff the map indicated there was a small cave, but it was close to the high tide line. Andy considered that the cave might be a place to hide out for the night. There was bonus money for how long he survived. A hundred thousand if he survived the first night, and another hundred grand if he survived twenty-four hours, until noon of tomorrow. Maybe he could at least leave Hattie and Kerry enough money so they wouldn't have to worry about the bills. If the viewing audience isn't happy that he does nothing this afternoon but hide out, screw 'em; a hundred grand is worth more than their boredom.

Of course, the Hunter may have thought of the same thing, and if he did, Andy would be trapped like a rat in the cave. Well, he decided, let's find it first, then we'll see.

Suddenly Andy stopped and stood still. He listened intently. The birds in the upper reaches of the rain forest had picked up their squawking, indicating they were fine with Andy's movements. If the Hunter was close to him, if that shot had not been just a wild attempt to scare him, then Andy wanted to know. He surveyed his surroundings, thick greenery wherever he looked. This scene was playing over to the viewers, he realized, or, maybe, at this moment, the camera has switched to the Hunter, who at this instant might have Andy in his rifle sights.

After what Andy estimated was five minutes, minutes during which the viewers and the producers were probably wondering what he was waiting for, Andy decided the Hunter was not near, and he continued his course, only this time he angled slightly northeast, to change the direction from which he would approach the cliff.

The rest had done him good. He continued to cut at the jungle flora and ignored the scratches he was accumulating as branches and vines grabbed at him as if he was their personal prey. The scratches on his arms drew more bugs and soon he wanted to scream from the irritation. Then he smelled it—water. He stopped and listened intently. He could hear the swoosh of waves hitting rocks; at least, Andy convinced himself that was what he heard.

It wasn't more than twenty-five yards more when the terrain changed. The ground sloped downward and the thick plant life gave way to grasses no higher than Andy's knees. He could see the water now, the Pacific Ocean, that much he knew, but for all he really knew, he could have been on one of the moons of Jupiter.

The slope became steeper and Andy stopped to rest and enjoy the panoramic scene of blue water, for as far as he could see. For a few seconds Andy forgot that this was a life or death scenario. *This might be the last beautiful sight I ever see!* As he continued his descent his foot slipped and he fell on his back. He began to slide downward and lost his knife. For some reason, rather than thinking about how he could stop his fall, he wondered if his helmet would come off, and if it did, would he be disqualified. Wouldn't they realize it was an accident? Couldn't they see on the screen?

"He's falling," Jan said. "He slipped on the path over on the east side, by the cliff."

"What the hell's he doing over there?" Colburn asked.

"He's just wandering, don't ya think? Even if he memorized the map, why would he go there?"

"Looks like he stopped," said Colburn. "No, he's sliding again. Shit, I hope he doesn't get hurt!"

"Why? Don't want to make it too easy for Hunter?" asked Jan Moore, one of the assistant producers.

"Yeah, well, what if breaks a leg and is just laying there? Is the Hunter going to kill him? That'd be kind of unsporting, don't ya think?"

"We have a plan for that," said Colburn. "Did you think we hadn't thought of that?"

"What plan?"

"The Hunter knows about it, but we've kept it quiet, until now," Colburn said. The producer grinned, a wicked grin made all the more evil looking by his thin eyebrows that curled upward from the corners of his eyes.

"If he has a shot at the Prey, Hunter can go for it, no problem. But if he has the Prey cornered, or wounded, we send a signal giving viewers a chance to vote on whether Hunter should kill the Prey, or let him live!"

"Good God! That's awful," said Jan.

In the background someone laughed, and someone else gasped. Jerry Osgood, the chief programmer, the only other person at the command site who had known of that possibility, stood up and smiled weakly.

Jan looked at him and opened her mouth, then closed it, then opened it, filled with anger but unable to form any words.

Finally she shouted, at both Colburn and Osgood. "You fiends! That's like the Romans, with their thumbs up or thumbs down! You're going to let the viewers decide if this man lives or dies! You'll all go to jail; we all will!"

Colburn laughed. "No one can touch us, Jan, relax. There's no law on this island except what we make it to be. Don't get holier-than-thou suddenly. You knew what this was about long ago, so don't pretend to be in anguish. It's too late for that."

He turned angry now, and was no longer smiling. "So sit down, watch the monitors, and think about what you'll do with your share of the ton of money we're making on this."

"Get a camera on him," added the producer.

"Yes sir, we have one in the trees right above him."

Jan slumped down into her chair, her eyes watching Andy lying at the bottom of the slope, panting for breath. She watched him rise up and saw him frantically searching for his knife. She saw the fear develop on his face as he realized that the one weapon he had, the

116

one thing that might give him a change to survive, was lost. She watched as he tried to scramble back up the slope, looking for the knife, but he only fell back and landed hard at the bottom of the slope.

The waves washed up to where Andy lay. The tide was going out now, so at least he wasn't going to drown, not yet, anyway. As he lay motionless Jan wondered if the man was unconscious or resting, or just frustrated and scared, ready to give up, and waiting for a quick death.

What was I thinking of when I got involved in this? I told myself this was just another 'reality show,' didn't I? For what they are paying me, or promised to pay, I found it easy to not ask more questions about how this was going to play out. I believed that in the end the Hunter would capture or corner the Prey, who would surrender, and we'd all go home happy.

Jan checked her other monitor, which showed the view from the Hunter's helmet/camera. His GPS location showed that he was at least five hundred yards from the Prey. That wasn't much distance but unless he had a good idea of where the Prey was, he could be a long time finding the poor sucker. How long would a viewing audience stayed tuned in, rapt by the thrill of seeing death happen on the screen? Not make-believe death, not special effects death, or even accidents shown on the news or Internet, where viewer discretion is warned. But real, as-it-happens bloody death, real time.

Andy slowly rose up on his arms. His face was dirty and sweaty and bloody. His arms were a mass of cuts and bruises and insect bites. His legs were lined with jagged scratches from his fall, thankfully not deep and not ones that bled much. Andy crawled into the water and let the ocean wash over him. The salt water stung as it lapped at his wounds, but Andy figured it would help to heal them. Anyway, right now, just lying here in the water felt good. *Might feel good to let the waves pull me out to sea.*

He actually fell asleep and all over the world, the viewers seeing the sand inches away from Andy's camera, his head down, not moving, wondered if he had died. But one of the long-range cameras revealed steady breathing, and of course the monitoring device in his arm also indicated he was alive, just sleeping. It was a good hour before Andy awoke, as much because his body sensed a change. The tide had gone out and the water no longer slapped at his body.

Andy looked to the west, across the Pacific, and saw that the sun was barely above the horizon. It would drop below in minutes and he'd be in complete darkness. Enormous black clouds were replacing the golden light and a cool breeze, a rather strong breeze, reminded Andy that he needed to find shelter. The developing coolness also reminded him that his clothes were soaking wet. I'd pay a thousand dollars for a towel and some dry clothes, Andy thought. And water! He now realized he'd also lost his backpack when he fell. All his food and water was gone and it was too dark to go looking for it. Ten thousand dollars I'd pay for a swig of sweet water!

Scanning the cliff side Andy noticed a structure at the top of the cliff, about fifty yards up. It was a small shack surrounded by fencing. Andy realized this was the electrified fence that surrounded the compound, which he was forbidden to enter. Before he could ascertain exactly what he was seeing the sun dipped under the horizon and the quickly developing darkness reminded Andy that he needed to find shelter.

Fortunately the cave he'd remembered seeing on the map was nearby. The ceiling was low; he had to stoop to get in and the cave was only about five feet deep and ten feet wide.

"Shit!" he exclaimed. "Call this a cave? Just a hole in the wall."

A flash of light jolted Andy. A second later a boom rumbled across the sea and sounded as if it ended right over Andy's head.

I'm all wet anyway, so what does it matter if it rains?

Andy plopped down on the damp ground inside the cave. Without food or water there wasn't anything to do except sit and think. Rest, that's good, because tomorrow I will surely die, and if I am alive, I won't stay in this cave and wait like a sheep to be killed.

Andy'd been told that his camera helmet had infrared red capability, so I guess insomniacs can stay up and watch the view from my head while I sleep. I wonder whereabouts the Hunter is now? Probably dry and cooking a dinner, drinking fresh water, or maybe they gave him cold beers. Hell, maybe at night they take him into the compound and he gets to sleep in bed! How the hell do I know?

Rain began to fall. Andy settled down on the ground, oblivious by now to the dampness. The only thing those assholes watching are going to see is the roof of the cave. He wasn't sleepy yet, after his nap, and his mind was active, thinking of many things, flitting from one subject to the other. He thought of his wife, and how stupid he'd been to treat her so badly. But then, I've been stupid all my life, haven't I?

Andy thought of an urgent reality: what do I do in the morning without a weapon? And can I find my backpack; can I even get back up the slope? This cave may be nice now, but the Hunter could easily trap me in here. And how far in does the tide come?

His eyes closed and his mind raced through thoughts of dying, and of living. The steady drum of the rain was soothing, and despite the more frequent cracks of thunder and the lightning flashes, sleep eventually overtook him.

Sometime during the night Andy was briefly awakened by a noise, a clatter that in a dreamy state he interpreted as a rockslide that had buried him in the cave. He imagined he smelled something burning, but whatever it was it couldn't burn long in this storm. He was too sleepy to think about it anymore.

The next time he neared consciousness he was dreaming that he was aboard a floundering rowboat, and amidst his concerns that the boat would overturn, he had to pee, badly. His eyes popped open as his face was splashed with salty water. A piece of kelp slapped him. He spat and sat up quickly, almost bumping his head on a cave roof. He and the ragged remains of his limited wardrobe were soaked. He felt warmth on his legs and realized that the dream had been partially real. The incoming tide was washing over Andy, cleansing him of the dirt and blood that had caked on him overnight. Now he needed to worry about drowning.

He exited the cave and surveyed his beach, or what was left of it. The tide was advancing quickly and soon he'd have no choice but to climb the cliff as high as needed.

His mouth craved water more than anything he'd ever craved before, more than any cold beer or swig of whiskey. His stomach gurgled with a gnawing that reminded Andy he hadn't eaten in over twelve hours and had lost his pack of supplies. He again smelled a faint odor of smoke, as if rubber or plastic was burning. An alien aroma amidst the fresh smell of rain, the salty sea, and the myriad fragrances of the jungle.

The water was now over his ankles. He felt something bump against him and at first thought it was a crab. But bouncy in the turf was a pot—a cooking pot! Confused, Andy picked it up and looked at it as if he'd never seen such a strange item. He looked out at the ocean assuming it was something that had drifted ashore having fallen off a ship, maybe a wreck that would send more debris to his beach. *His* beach, yeah.

Then he saw more things on the shore and his brain recalled the noise he had heard during the night. He looked up to the top of the cliff and saw a break in the fence. The storage shed had crumpled in the storm, maybe hit by lightning, and pushed against the fence. From there downward was a trail of objects that had broken through the fence and tumbled down, some of the items reaching the bottom. As Andy looked around him he began to spot more things bouncing in the waves, some being pulled out, then thrown back in towards shore.

Mostly they were kitchen utensils: pots, spatulas and other objects he couldn't give a name to, a colander, more pans, even a few kitchen knives. He grabbed as many items as could hold in one arm and began to climb the cliff. As he got closer to the top he could see what had happened.

The edge of the cliff had slowly eroded away, this latest storm being the coup de grace. Without adequate support the shed and the fence had slipped. Eventually the fence had broken, the shed had slipped farther and its contents had spilled onto the cliff. Maybe the electricity had been shorted out in this section by the storm, and no alarm had been raised yet, or noticed. Or maybe it had been noticed and someone would be here soon to fix the fence.

Whatever, Andy felt the first hint of hope. These items might be used as weapons or protection against the Hunter, who surely would find him today. When the tide went out, the Hunter would have access to Andy's cave. Andy could stay here and wait, a sitting duck, or return to the main body of the island and continue to scramble for his life. Neither prospect was inviting.

Why did this seem like a good idea at one time? Oh yeah, jail, bills, a broken marriage, it all comes back to me now.

"Is he still at the cave site?" asked Colburn, watching the view from Andy's helmet.

"Yeah, the GPS says so," replied an assistant.

"So where is he getting this stuff he's picking up? Looks like he's got pots and pans."

"Just a sec…"

"Oh, yeah, that's over on the east side…there's some kind of storage shed there."

"What?!" Colburn screamed. "You mean he broke in?"

"No way, boss," a man named Teasdale said. "He couldn't have climbed up the cliff. Besides, the fence is electrified, and the alarm would have gone off if he'd broken in."

"Could there be a short? Check on that, now!" Colburn yelled out. "And switch to the Hunter's view."

Bracing himself against a narrow ledge, his arms trying to hold on to his treasures, Andy watched as the tide flowed onto the beach and higher up the side of the cliff. It was too steep to climb higher, and the sides of the wall were beginning to crumble. Rather than hard rock the cliff appeared to be more like a clay which wasn't going to resist the force of the waves for very long. Maybe a few days, Andy thought, long after I'm gone.

From his perch Andy watched the water roll in until he noticed it seemed to have peaked and was no longer rising. Every third or fourth wave splashed him but the water level was definitely holding and maybe receding. He'd have to cling here for the time being; it would be awhile before the water had flowed out enough to uncover the beach and allow him an easy path out of the cove.

Few of the worldwide audience had noted the view from the Prey as he was climbing the cliff. His head had been moving too much to give a clear picture and the control booth had switched to a view from the Hunter before people could figure out what Andy was doing.

From the Hunter's view the audience saw him as he moved along a path, then slow his pace as the path turned sharply downhill. Viewers who monitored the GPS signals on the Internet realized that the Hunter was close on the tail of his quarry. Anxiety and beer sales increased.

The Hunter stopped and surveyed the area. He calculated that he'd need to carefully balance himself as he climbed downward and the Prey might try to ambush him here and turn the tables. But the foliage was sparse and it would be difficult for him to hide. If I'm right, the Hunter thought, this leads to the beach, and I don't think he'll have many places to hide there, other than the small cave. I can finish this job this morning. I just hope I can get a shot from a reasonable distance; close up, I'm not sure I could do it, he admitted to himself. That would be too much like murder in cold blood.

The Hunter inched his way along the steep path, slippery from the rain, setting each foot down slowly, after each step bracing himself against a slip on the muddy trail. Several feet off the trail and too far away to reach, was a pack back. It had to be the Prey's! The Prey had probably lost it going down the path last night and he couldn't find it in the dark. Next to the pack the Hunter saw a shiny object: a knife! The poor sap's lost everything and he's trapped on the beach!

Above the beach, clinging to the cliff above the cave, Andy heard noises. There was an entire catalog of sounds to interpret: birds singing or calling out warnings; the waves, gentle now, washing quietly ashore and back out, each time taking more of the tide with it; pebbles and clods of clay slipping down the cliff, the metallic groan of the fence as it lost more of its footing, scaring Andy that the entire cliff would crash down on him.

But amongst those sounds was one less natural than those of the jungle and its inhabitants. It was a scraping sound, a raw sound to Andy's ear. It came from the direction of the path, the only route to the beach and the cove, and Andy's simple hideout of a cave. It was the Hunter, Andy knew.

He should have been thinking desperately what to do, but for a moment Andy wondered if it was prime time in America, where RealDrama was getting its largest audience. Had it been planned this way?

Andy edged his way down the cliff, trying to be quiet, and stepped in the water, which was still over his ankles. If he crawled

124

back into the cave, the Hunter might think Andy wasn't anywhere on the beach, and would leave. Still, he'd seen the map too, and he had to be thinking that the cave would have made a nice overnight stop. He might also have seen the items Andy had dropped along the way.

No, Andy decided, offense is my best choice. Some offense: he looked at his sad collection. A colander, two small pots, a steak knife-- his only real weapon, a potato peeler and a spatula. He couldn't carry any more items even if he wanted to.

If he returned to the cave, he wouldn't have room to maneuver; the Hunter could just shoot into the cave and end the suspense. If he tried to stand up to the Hunter, pots and pans versus a high-powered rifle, the result would be the same, only out in the open where millions of salivating idiots would have a great view of the final act of their show.

What the hell can I do, catch bullets with a pot?

What if I attacked? Uphill, sloshing in water, what chance would I have?

Andy definitely smelled fire now. He looked up towards where the storage shed hung precariously, pushing more and more against the broken fence. Something had caught on fire and has been smoldering. He could see a sliver of orange frame coming from inside the damaged shed. The least of my problems.

Now he heard a definite sound of something moving, and it was near. Andy felt panic rising. Oh God, get me out of this, even without the money, and I'll be good! I'll get a job, I won't drink anymore, I'll be good to my wife; I really don't want to die, not for any money! Amazing how impending disaster can cure a person of his wasteful ways!

Think, dummy, think! You've got to do something!

Andy could hear the crackling flames and feel their heat as they found fuel and burst into the trees that lined the top of the cliff. They were spreading at lightning speed, and surely the audience, and the fools in the control booth, would see them from the cameras stationed around.

The orange flames began to roar and treetops exploded. Andy didn't even hear the shot; he just felt the wind speed by his face and a chunk of rock ricochet off his shoulder. He thought he'd been hit by a bullet.

The control booth was in disarray. Colburn was yelling at everyone.

"Where's that fire at?! Why isn't someone taking care of it?!"

"It's at the far end of the island. It's hard to get to."

"I don't care if it's on the goddamn moon, get someone to put it out before the whole fuckin' island burns down!"

"Switch to the Hunter! See, he's got the Prey in his sights! Now, split screen so we can see both views."

Just as the camera went to a split screen Andy ducked down, though there wasn't much to hide behind. He couldn't see the Hunter but knew he was there. *What the hell do I do?*

Above him, and spreading towards the point where the path began its descent towards the beach, the fire was speeding from branch to branch, jumping the trees faster than the most talented monkey in the jungle. Behind him, a dead end of crumbling cliff and the endless sea. There was only one direction to go.

Andy dropped his pots and pans and the other items. Then he took off his shorts. He put the colander on his hand, balancing on the camera-helmet but not obstructing the view. He picked up his pans and knife and other gadgets, took a deep breath, and then charged up the path, screaming as loud as he could.

Ahead of him, coming down the path, the Hunter heard Andy's scream and froze. What the hell? An instant later he saw a naked man with something on his head and carrying pots and pans come running at him. The Hunter gaped in shock. His camera sent the picture to the world.

"What the hell, he's naked!" someone yelled in the control booth while Colburn looked at the screen in glee. Then he began to laugh.

"This is great! I couldn't imagine anything better!"

In homes and in sports bars and wherever Internet access was available people gazed in amazement at the stupefying view of Andrew Jones, naked except for his shoes and a colander on his head, screaming his fool head off, running towards the screen. In a few select Imax theatres 3D viewers jumped as if they themselves were about to be shot.

Although some viewers were laughing, all were stunned, and in no time the audience realized the man was going to be killed in front of their eyes. There were those who cheered gleefully, who couldn't wait to see it, real blood, not that phony stuff you get in the movies, that never looks genuine. But many others suddenly thought, what are we doing, watching this, accepting it?

On RealDrama Island the Hunter recovered from his initial shock and raised his rifle, but he lost his footing and slipped at the moment he fired. A bullet hit one of Andy's pots and knocked it out of his hand. The Prey almost fell over, but caught himself and continued his charge. The Hunter had fallen down into a sitting position.

Andy threw a pot at the Hunter who ducked and raised an arm in defense. Andy threw his last pot, which hit the Hunter on the elbow and caused him to drop the rifle. Andy threw his spatula and was about to throw the knife just as he reached the Hunter, who cringed in fear.

The viewers now saw Andy standing above the Hunter holding a small knife, while the split screen view showed the Hunter covering himself with his arm. Then they saw the view from Andy's helmet as he looked up the path. The entire jungle appeared to be ablaze. In the 3D theatres the flicking flames caused people to flinch.

Andy reached towards the Hunter, who accepted his hand and with Andy's help, stood up. Andy gazed at him, seeing for the first time the face of a man who for a million dollars had planned to kill him.

"It's over, eh? A tie?"

The Hunter nodded. "We better get outta here. Where's your pants?"

Andy looked towards the beach. "Too late to get them."

"Well, if you meant to startle me, it worked."

Andy tore the helmet off his head and tossed it down the path and watched it fall for as far as he could watch it. The audience saw the trail and grasses flip over and over as the camera helmet rolled downhill. The Hunter took off his helmet, looked at it as if he was shocked that he'd been wearing it, and emitted a soft grunt. Then he tossed it down the slope. The two men scurried up the path, helping each other. At the top they saw a jeep carrying three men approach them. For a moment both Hunter and Prey thought they'd be killed.

"Goddamit!" screamed Colburn. "No one gets any money! They both defaulted!"

"I'm glad," said Jan. "Good for them."

"You're fired," yelled Colburn. "You're all fired!"

One man got out of the jeep. He handed Andy a pair of shorts and bottles of water to both Andy and the Hunter.

"We've got to evacuate the island. The fire's spreading towards the control booth and we don't have enough equipment to fight it. C'mon, we'll take you to a boat."

"That's fine, boss," said Jan. "I think we're all out of job for now anyway. We need to get out of here before this place burns down. C'mon."

Jan tugged on her boss's arm while he stayed glued to the computer screen.

"Goddamit," said Colburn, not yelling anymore. "This could have been a great show, goddamit."

*

"The Blue Blouse"

The only thing wrong with Jacqueline was that I met her two months before I was supposed to marry Cynthia. Everybody else called her Jackie, I soon discovered, but I always loved the sound of her full name, Jacqueline.

I don't remember what book it was that I held in my hand when we first met; I've strained my brain trying to remember but it's no use.

"Have you got a light?" she asked.

I turned towards the sound, not sure if the question was posed at me. I peered into the deep blue sea. Two large eyes, dark blue and glistening as if teary, peeked at me over the glasses that the woman tipped downward with a finger. Equally attractive was the blouse she wore. It was a shade lighter than her eyes, not quite the cobalt blue sky we sometimes see on a perfectly clear day. It was the softer shade of blue when the sky is strewn with scattered white pillows. One pearl button decorated the front of the blouse, at her neck, the cloud in the sky, so to speak. It appeared to be more decorative than functional so I assumed the blouse buttoned up in the back. Amidst the grays and browns of the bookshelves and dim yellow light, the blouse was the sea and the sky, her eyes a beacon from a lighthouse, guiding weary sailors to a safe haven. Okay, so I was a frustrated poet.

"Uh, no," I said, uselessly putting my free hand in my pocket, looking for something I knew wasn't there.

"That's okay," she said. "You didn't think I smoked, did you?"

Back then; many people did, before we were warned smoking could kill.

I looked down at the open book I held in my left hand, thinking our conversation was over.

"So what are you reading?" she asked.

I had no idea; my mind on her, not the book. In retrospect I feel like I stood there, tongue-tied, for several minutes, amazed that she was still here. Surely it was only a few seconds. She was very pretty, maybe beautiful. She smelled fresh, a sharp contrast to the musty odor of the bookstore. It was one of those wonderful, dusty, old bookstores in Hollywood that I often frequented on a Friday night after work. I'd roam in and out of the rooms and the aisles, eventually creeping upstairs where it was quiet except for the occasional creak of the worn floorboards, or the turning of a page from a fellow browser. I'd climbed the stairs with anticipation, wondering what treasure I would find. Or a nugget; it didn't have to be anything fabulous, just something new to me.

The woman's long hair looked and smelled like it had been recently shampooed; it glistened in the pale light of the naked overhead bulbs and I had the urge to run my hand through it. Nothing sexual about the thought, not yet, anyway.

"You don't remember me, do you?" she asked, her voice low-pitched and sounding slightly hoarse. At first I thought she was sick, or forcing a voice she thought was sexy. A few years later her voice would become famous.

I shook my head, my brain working feverishly to remember where we'd met.

"Dan and Cheryl's party, last Halloween. I was dressed as Cleopatra. You said you wished you'd come as Marc Antony."

I shook my head ever so lightly. "No, sorry, I don't know a Dan and Cheryl, but I wish I thought of that comeback."

"Oh, sorry, I guess I mistook you for someone else."

"That's okay, I'm glad you did." There it was, I was flirting with her.

"The truth is, I'm an actress rehearsing a part. One of my assignments is to walk up to a stranger and say my lines, and based on the response, try to stay in character as long as possible."

"How's it going so far?"

She shrugged. "The first two guys I tried it on offered to take me to dinner and buy me a carton of cigarettes."

"I guess I'd better come up with a new line," I said with a smile. At least, I hoped it came out as a smile, not a stupid grin.

She smiled back, and suddenly I forget what Cynthia looked like.

Two hours later we were still talking, now in the coffee shop across from the bookstore. A package of cigarettes lay on the table between us, put there by Jacqueline shortly after we sat down, and untouched since then. We'd been engrossed in conversation and other than coffee, several cups by now, hadn't paid attention to anything but each other.

"Are those just a prop?" I asked when I finally noticed the package.

"Oh," she was startled at the realization the cigarettes were there.

"No, not just...I smoke occasionally. You?" she picked up the package and handed it to me. I shook out a cigarette and offered it to her. I hadn't had anything to drink but coffee, yet I was drunk, mesmerized by her eyes and her voice.

She shook her head. "No, there's enough smoke from the others," she said, nodding out into the room, where a blue-gray haze hung overhead. Ever after I would think how weird it was that she and I both quit smoking at the same time, something Cynthia had been bugging me to do. It was as if Jacqueline's acting assignment, asking a stranger for a light, jarred us and made our introduction to each other a point that had to be marked for evermore by *not* smoking. Some of her roles in movies or on stage would require Jacqueline to smoke, but except for while acting, she never smoked, at least not around me, and she said not otherwise, either. For me it became a badge of honor, recognition of how we met. I could never tell anyone, ever, how it came about that I quit smoking, or what gave me the strength to resist when people around me were puffing away. It was silly, yet I clung to our secret, like a pact, one to keep until the day when…when, I didn't know.

"I love your blouse," I said. "It's a spectacular color."

"Thank you, but I over-dressed for hanging around old book stores trying my lines on strangers. It's the most expensive article of clothing I own."

"It's almost as beautiful as…"

"Close your eyes, Joe."

"Huh?"

"Just close them, please."

I did as she asked.

"What color are my eyes?" she asked.

"Well, blue, deep blue, darker than your blouse. I figure your wore that blouse because it seems to contrast and at the same time blend with your eyes." I shrugged. "Heck, I don't know anything about clothes or colors."

"Hmm. Pretty good, Joe. Most people notice the blouse when I wear it, but not the color of my eyes. Now keep your eyes closed."

In my mind I visualized how she looked, much clearer to me now than Cynthia, whom I had known for three years.

"What color is my hair?"

"That's easy. It's creamy, midnight black, long and silky."

"God! What are you, an amateur poet?"

I laughed, feeling slightly silly, but having fun. "Amateur? You mean that wasn't good?"

"Okay, you like my blouse, how many buttons are there?"

I shrugged. "None in front, I haven't had a chance to check the back. Oh, yes, you have a pearl button at the top, at your throat, but I think it's only decorative."

"That's good, Joe. You do pay attention. You can open your eyes."

"What was that all about?"

"It's a device I use on myself, to see how observant I am of the people around me. It helps me to respond to the other actors. As for this blouse, I'm going to put it away and save it for a very special occasion."

"I hope I see you wear it again," I said. At the same time I thought, what the hell are you doing, Joseph?

Fortunately for me, Cynthia always worked the night shift on Fridays so she didn't expect to hear from me, which is why I was out prowling the used book stores until the midnight hour, or later, on Fridays. Sometimes I hit a movie; tonight I was glad I'd opted for the bookstore. When the coffee shop closed Jacqueline and I moved to a bar and drank more coffee, to the point where we were beginning to feel a caffeine high, but maybe it was only our infatuation with each other.

In a movie or a novel we would end up in bed, having known each other for a few hours, enough, by fiction's standards, to move on to physical intimacy. I was too involved with Cynthia to even consider sex with someone else right then, a foolish belief, I found out less than a month later. By then I'd suggested we delay the wedding, an episode too ugly to talk about. So when intimacy did occur, I felt a little less guilty than I probably deserved to feel. But it seemed like the right thing to do at the time, that is, call off the wedding, using the time honored cliché that maybe we 'should take a little more time, until we're sure.'

"Don't give me that cold feet line, sweetheart," Cynthia said. Bitterness spewed out of her voice and she made no attempt to disguise her disgust. But I'm getting ahead of myself; that's for another chapter of my life.

The bar closed at two a.m. and I hoped Cynthia hadn't tried to call me. She knew my favorite bookstores all closed by midnight.

Jacqueline had taken a bus to get to Hollywood so I offered to drive her home, an apartment she shared in Glendale with two other hopeful starlets. Neither of her roommates ever made it in show business, other than a commercial or two, and in fact I only met them once. Jacqueline, of course, did achieve fame and fortune, using the stage name, 'Jackie James', because 'Jacqueline Donaldson' was too long and not 'engaging enough', her agent insisted.

"So, ah, maybe we can get together again," I suggested, as we sat in my car outside her apartment.

"Sure," she answered quickly. She sat close to the window, as if eager to get out, or at least not willing to let me get too close. I took that as a sign that a goodnight kiss wasn't in order. After all, it wasn't like we'd been on a date. And I was an engaged man, for cryin' out loud! Not that Jacqueline knew; I'd carefully avoided the topic of on-going relationships during our hours of conversation.

"Next Friday?" I suggested, mentally ticking off what errands Cynthia and I had to attend to next week to prepare for the wedding.

"Sure, Friday? Old books and gallons of coffee?" she said with a smile.

"Maybe some food this time? Or a movie? Do actresses go to movies?"

"Of course they do; I love movies. Let's meet at the bookstore, okay?"

"I could pick you up, no problem. About seven?"

"You're on," She deftly leaned over and kissed me on the cheek, opened the door and scooted up the walk, waving back at me. When she reached the door she turned and threw me a kiss. I waved back and waited until she had unlocked the door and gone inside. I sat there in the car for a full minute re-living this evening, and thinking maybe I wasn't ready to get married yet. I'm only twenty-eight. Yeah, and Cynthia is twenty-seven and eager to start a family, who am I kidding, *only* twenty-eight. If not now, to Cynthia, when? Just because I met a pretty face, an actress, one of thousands in Hollywood, each one thinking they'll be the next big star? No one, no matter how attractive, should have affected me the way Jacqueline did if I was truly ready to marry Cynthia. I drove home, desperately trying to remember Cynthia's face.

On Saturdays Cynthia and I usually spent the entire day together. I called in sick. Naturally she insisted she'd come over and take care of me, and I insisted just as vociferously that I didn't want her to catch my cold. Actually, I suggested I might have Black Water Fever, a rare disease usually contracted by drinking water from rivers in East Africa.

"I don't know where I could have caught it, but the coffee tasted lousy last night."

"Dear, I'm sure you don't have Black Fever, or whatever you said. Now stay in bed and I'll be by after I do my errands. I was so hoping you could come with me to look at drapes."

That made me feel better—I would escape shopping for drapes. Playing sick now didn't seem so awful, even though I was doing it because my mind was on Jacqueline and I was already looking forward to next Friday night. What a rat I am!

I called Mack, my old Army buddy. He would tell me what to do.

"Sure, go for it," he advised, after I told him about my pending date with Jacqueline.

"You're not married yet, Joe. Sow some oats."

"Yeah, Mack, but I am engaged."

"Didn't I tell you? What did I say, huh, huh?"

"Yeah, yeah, it's easy for you to say, you've been burned before."

"And learned my lesson, too. No more long-term entanglements, not for this guy. Hey, Joe, if you break up with Cynthia, mind if I give her a call?"

"Goodbye, Mack. Thanks for nothing." I slammed the phone down.

Now I actually felt sick; I'd brought it on myself by guilt and worry. By the time Cynthia got to my place I was sneezing and had a headache. Mind over matter, or something, whatever the hell that means. So this lovely lady I was due to marry—after I cheated on her this Friday—brought me a pillow from the bedroom to the couch, fixed me soup, and rubbed my feet. Well, at least she wouldn't expect to cuddle up to me, so I wouldn't feel like more of a creep than I already did.

And yet, I couldn't stop thinking about Jacqueline.

A lot of years have passed, and it's difficult now to remember what that week was like, from Saturday when I played sick to the point I really did feel ill, and Cynthia babied me, to the following Friday. I know that I struggled with how to suggest that we delay the wedding. More and more plans were being finalized and the longer I waited the more difficult it was going to be. Then I decided I'd wait to see how my date with Jacqueline went. Maybe I'd find that the original fascination with her was a passing fancy, nothing more. Maybe in the light of reason and calmness she'd even look ugly.

I do remember that I couldn't concentrate on my work all week. When Friday came I rushed home after work, shaved, showered and slapped on a new after shave, one I'd never tried before, nervous as rookie in his first at bat in front of the home fans, then dashed out to the car and forget where my keys were. I worried that I'd be late to pick up Jacqueline and tore the apartment apart trying to find the keys. They were in the door.

As it was I had plenty of time so I stopped at the bookstore where we had met the previous Friday. I browsed the racks, not seeing anything I was looking at, checking my watch every minute. I didn't want to be late, but I didn't want to be over-eagerly early. When I arrived at her apartment I sat in the car until one minute before seven, palms sweating, unsure what we were going to do. I hadn't given it much thought, I'd been so nervous. Dinner? A movie? I went to the door and knocked.

She wasn't ugly. She made the sweater she was wearing look like the sexiest piece of clothing ever invented or worn by a human female. I gasped.

"Look at my eyes, Joe, my blue eyes," Jacqueline said.

"Oh, yeah, sorry; how are you?" I stammered.

She laughed and took my arm. "Shall we go? Do you have a plan?"

"If you aren't hungry yet, I thought a movie first."

"Good, I want to see *Butterfield 8,* with Elizabeth Taylor. I heard she is so good that she may win an Oscar."

"Fine with me," I said.

Taylor did win an Oscar for her performance, and I remember watching Jacqueline as she watched Taylor on the screen. I knew then that this is what she wanted more than anything, to act, to make it in movies as an actress. I also knew that Jacqueline would succeed, and anything she and I had going now was ephemeral. Looking at her, fascinated by the performance on the screen, I realized that with Cynthia I had the makings of stability, of being with someone who wanted me for all time, that I would come first, not second to a career. Jacqueline was going places, and I wasn't going to go with her.

As spellbound as Jacqueline was by the performance on screen, so was I by her, and I didn't have the strength to immediately break off our embryonic relationship. I was determined to enjoy the ride as long as I could stretch it out, using the excuse that it would help me to know if I was ready to be a permanent husband to Cynthia. The way we can rationalize, amazing, isn't it!

I continued to see her, every Friday, a ritual I came to look forward to so quickly I couldn't remember what my Friday evenings had been like just a few weeks ago. Then we managed to see each other on Sunday afternoons, when Cynthia and her mother had to take care of 'wedding things', as Cynthia told me. I shut my mind off, knowing I was being a rat for not telling them to quit planning because there wasn't going to be any wedding.

And yet, deep down I knew Jacqueline wasn't ready to commit to me, and I didn't know exactly what I was ready to commit to. If I ended the relationship with Cynthia, did that necessarily mean Jacqueline and I would develop a long term one? I was so confused I seriously considered two ideas, which in the light of decades later, seems so silly I can't believe I gave either of them a moment's consideration. One was to run away from home! Yes, at my age, with a good job, ready to start a family, I was going to drop out of sight, not say anything to anybody I knew; sure. The second idea was to ask

142

Jacqueline to marry me. What we would do then, I had no idea, not if she held ambitions of a career in movies.

Basically though, I had convinced myself I was sowing my last wild oats, I had a right to, and I was going to do it. But slowly—well, not so slowly I felt I was falling in love with Jacqueline and out of love with Cynthia.

I try to forget the episode where I suggested to Cynthia we call off the wedding; I believe I commented on that earlier, and her angry response. Can you blame her? We parted with her crying and on the phone to her mother. I felt sick, called Cynthia as soon as I got home, and we made up over the phone. At least she made up. Now I had to figure out how to break it off with Jacqueline, and I felt worse about hurting her than I did Cynthia; odd, isn't it?

It was Sunday, only six days before the wedding, and I wrestled with how to tell Jacqueline I couldn't see her next Friday. I'd have to tell her I was going to a wedding rehearsal. Oh wonderful, she'd say, who's getting married? Well, I am, on Saturday—have I told you about Cynthia?—which will probably put a crimp on next Sunday afternoon. Slap! Jesus, what a coward I am; now I was cheating on two women! That was what I imagined; here is what really happened.

We were to meet at our favorite nook, grab a snack, see a movie, whichever one Jacqueline chose, and then have a late dinner. My new idea was for me to go to her place, skip the movie, and snuggle in for the evening. But I couldn't get a hold of her all day and when I'd talk to her earlier in the week she said she'd be too busy to go home after work, so to meet at the coffee shop. This was in those primitive days before cell phones.

As soon as I saw her I knew something was up. Her smile was there, the hug was genuine, but the spark was missing. My heart skipped as I was sure she had found out about Cynthia before I had the chance to tell her. Remembering back, I honestly think that right up until the time we met that evening, I wasn't sure if I was going to ask her to marry me or tell her I was getting married next week. Or, rotten to the core, plan to make love to her tonight and tell her in the morning. The instant I saw her I knew I couldn't do the latter, as much as I wanted to hold and kiss her for as long as I could, and put off the inevitable.

"How was your day?" I said, worried that I didn't know the answer in advance.

"It was good, Joe...but also, maybe not so good."

"Hmm. Kinda like most days, hey, some good some bad."

"You want the good news or the bad news?" she asked.

Here it comes, she's found out.

"Ah, do you want to order something first? Are we going to have time to eat before the movie? What do you want to see?" I rattled off several questions, stalling for time, to what end, who knows?

"Gosh, Joe, you seem nervous? Are you afraid of what I have to say?"

"Well, yeah, kind of."

"Let me give you what I think is the good news first."

Then it hit me. "Oh, and from the good I can then figure out what the bad news is, right?"

She smiled and shrugged.

She opened her mouth to speak, hesitated, then said quickly, "I've got a part, a definite part in a Broadway production. Not a big

144

part, but a dozen lines and several minutes on stage. I have to be there in three days."

I should have been happy for her. I was happy for her. This was what she wanted. "Great, Jacqueline, what wonderful news! But what's bad, I mean, it doesn't mean you'll never come back from New York, does it?" I knew the answer, in fact, this would make it easier. I wouldn't even have to tell her about Cynthia.

"My agent says that if this job pans out, he can definitely get me more work in New York. He's got two other roles almost locked up for me. Later, maybe I'll come back to Hollywood to make movies. Joe, this is what I want, more than anything, you know?"

More than me. I nodded, torn between emotions I couldn't adequately describe, somewhere between despair and relief.

"Well, that is…good news, of course. I can't wait to see you on the big screen! So, we have to celebrate", I added, putting my best foot forward. What I really wanted to do was hug her and not let her go until the sun came up. Knowing it would be the last time, she was thinking along the same lines.

"I arranged for the apartment to be free. It'll take a few minutes to get the messy kitchen organized but I thought we'd have a celebratory dinner there. I'm not a bad cook, you know. And there's no hurry, we have all night…unless…unless you'd rather stay here, where we first got to know each other."

"Oh no, we should celebrate. Let's go." The last thing I wanted to do was sit here and brood.

I never went back to that coffee shop, nor the bookstore. Jacqueline and I talked all evening about her hopes for a career, and that, who knows, maybe some day we might get together again. Then she added that she didn't expect me to wait for her. Many years later I told Jacqueline I had seriously considered asking her to marry me, even though I was only a week away from marrying someone else. By then enough time had passed that she could laugh it off, though she would reprimand me for my rascally behavior.

Her announcement was a shock to my system, delayed, of course, until after I left her near dawn on Monday morning. I knew I'd miss her, yet I also knew that had I broken up with Cynthia, it wasn't going to change Jacqueline's mind about going to New York. I'd be here, she'd be there, and Cynthia would be crushed. And she had a big, I mean *big*, brother, who wouldn't have taken kindly to my jilting his darling sister.

No, it wasn't easy, don't ever think it was. It took me until the rehearsal dinner on Friday to begin to remember how much I cared for Cynthia, to look forward again to being with her, to building a life and family with her. I did quite well, I felt, in clearing my mind of Jacqueline. I told myself I'd been a fool to jeopardize my engagement to Cynthia. The next few years flew by and I was reminded of Jacqueline only briefly, when I went to see her first movie. She had a nice part, did well, I thought, and looked gorgeous. I guess she had some other parts soon after, but I forgot to keep track until her big break came.

I always enjoyed movies, Cynthia less so. Jacqueline's break-through role came in a movie called *Deadly Loves,* which was a bit of a tearjerker and not the type of movie I'd normally go see. But when

Cynthia asked me to take her she was surprised that I agreed so readily.

Jacqueline's role was, not ironically, similar to Taylor's role in *Butterfield 8*. We were still in a time where characters, especially female ones, who did bad things in movies, had to pay a price. Jacqueline's character had stolen another woman's husband, leading to tragic consequences for several people. Even though the character didn't know the man was married until after she was in love with him, and after he had promised to marry her, she, like a character out of Dickens, had to bear the punishment to cleanse everyone else. It was a sad role, but Jacqueline performed it magnificently. While discussing the movie I neglected to mention that I had known Jackie James. I didn't think I could explain when I knew her without hemming and hawing.

I was befuddled beyond belief when a few days after the Academy Award nominations were announced, and Jacqueline was on the list, a woman describing herself as Jackie James' personal secretary called and said Miss James was inviting me and my family to the Academy Award Presentation show, and would we be coming and how many tickets did we need.

It took me awhile to explain that I had indeed once known Jackie James, very briefly I pointed out, (which was true), but I hadn't recognized her because of her name change (which was not true).

Cynthia and I decided to make an adventure of it and left the kids with a sitter overnight, went to a show the night before the Awards ceremony, stayed at an expensive hotel in downtown Los Angeles, and spent an entire month's food budget on dinner. We left the Academy Awards for the climax. We'd also been invited to Miss

James' private party following the show, but as yet had not actually talked to her, much to my chagrin. I began to worry that the whole purpose of this was for Jacqueline to reveal to Cynthia my duplicity, but that just shows how little I understood Jacqueline.

When we arrived we were ushered backstage to meet Jacqueline, or Miss James, if you must. When I first saw her I was stunned. Rather than a new dress Jacqueline was wearing the blue blouse she had worn the first time we met. She had told me she would not wear it again until a special occasion arose. Of course, I had no way of knowing whether she had worn it since, but the look she gave in response to the surprise on my face told me she hadn't. Yes, it was old, and had anyone known how old she would either have been ridiculed, or praised for maintaining so well a classic piece of wardrobe. She looked spectacular.

After staring for a moment I introduced her to Cynthia and somehow managed to hold it together when Jacqueline hugged me and gave me a kiss on the cheek. I knew Cynthia was wondering how well we'd know each other.

But her show of affection was more in my mind than an actual flirtation; she was perfectly proper. I truly believed at the time that whatever she had felt for me had long since dissipated, as well it should have. She'd already been married once, though the marriage only lasted a year, and now she was certainly one of the most glamorous and desired actresses in the world.

Cynthia didn't want to be left out of our small talk so she offered the observation that I hadn't recognized Jackie in the movie because of her name change. Jacqueline didn't bat an eye and remarked that it had been several years since we'd run into each other at some old bookstore. If I recall, she said, you bought me a cup of coffee.

I'm not sure what Cynthia suspected but she never made any accusations or tried to pry. Possibly it was because of Jacqueline's personality; despite being beautiful and famous, surely a threat to any red-blooded man who wasn't blind, she made all people, even wives and girl friends, at ease around her. She never came on to me, even in joking, and despite fame and beauty, never became a target of the gossips. She was boring, one gossip columnist criticized.

We remained fans of Jacqueline's movies thereafter and stayed in contact, mostly with birthday and Christmas cards. Cynthia was actually disappointed when we weren't invited to Jacqueline's second wedding.

"We aren't actually her dear friends, Cyn."

"Well, still, it would have been fun, and we could have told our friends all about it."

I was glad we weren't invited. Three years later I went through another round of mixed emotions when Jacqueline's second marriage also failed.

Don't get me wrong, I wasn't constantly pining for her. I didn't feel I was in love with her anymore, it was more a case of the fascination of knowing a famous person, and having at one time been rather intimate with her, but not being able to tell anyone. Our friends were aghast that we had gone to the Academy Awards and the guys teased hell out of me, trying to get me to tell all. I insisted I hardly remembered her and absorbed the insults that there must be something wrong with me. Maybe was I getting too, you know, hollywoodish, heh, heh!

No way was I going to brag about my short affair with an Academy Award winning actress. It would have soiled what we had shared and the renewed friendship we now enjoyed.

After her second marriage failed Jacqueline went into seclusion and didn't make a movie for over two years. Again we were surprised when she invited us, and the kids, to a home she had built in the New Hampshire woods. Cynthia and the kids were more exited than I was, not that I was blasé to the idea of seeing Jacqueline again.

Over the next few years we grew more comfortable with each other and Cynthia and I became friends with Jacqueline and her small circle of close friends. She even came to our house a few times, though we never let the neighbors know and we only went out in the evening, Jacqueline wearing big hats and dark glasses.

I never thought I'd outlive Cynthia, much less two wives. The brain tumor struck her like a bullet out of nowhere. Jacqueline showed up at Cynthia's funeral, to the shock of the guests. Her appearance at the funeral subjected her to the stares of people who forgot why they were where they were.

"I probably shouldn't have come, Joe, The people are looking at me instead of thinking about Cynthia. I'm sorry, I didn't think."

I hugged her and told it was all right and that we should keep in touch. She gave me a timid hug, we talked for a few minutes, and she apologized that she couldn't stay longer because she had left the movie set in a lurch when she heard the news. How she heard I never did find out.

I didn't see her again for over two years, although we did send a few messages, light correspondence, without either of us saying anything of real substance; testing the waters, so to speak. I guess she was waiting for me, and I, quite truly, hardly thought of her for over a year after Cynthia passed. Then I waited longer, probably wasting time we could have had together, before I called.

It was easier for me to visit her, in her secluded hideaway, and little by little I spent more and more of my time in New Hampshire. The kids were grown and developing their own lives now so I was pretty much on my own. For my first few visits I stayed in the guest suite.

Jacqueline hated the limelight by then and worked sparingly, preferring to spend most of her time in her comfort zone, this old brick house in the woods of New Hampshire, far away from Hollywood and New York. She wrote a book about her days in the movie world but it didn't have any racy revelations about her leading men, so it didn't sell well.

Her socialization was limited to a small group, none of whom were famous actors or actresses. Mostly they were behind the scenes people and I found them to be regular and genuine people, albeit a bit richer than the average guy on the street. The phonies and groupies had long been weeded out of Jacqueline's life.

There was a sense of loneliness about her I'd never noticed before. I can't speak of any romances she might have had, but obviously her two attempts at marriage had failed. She wasn't acting much anymore, but took a few supporting roles when it was one she found especially interesting, and I got to hang around the set as if I was a VIP. She'd arrange for me to be an executive producer, just for the fun of getting my name on the screen. My kids got more of a thrill out of it than I did.

Joe junior and Jenny still couldn't believe how we had hooked up. Finally I admitted to them that I had briefly dated Jacqueline before she was a movie star, but I hadn't told their mother because I was afraid she'd be jealous. But I was firm in explaining that nothing had gone on with Jacqueline and I while their mother and I were married.

And I didn't say I had usually seen her pictures two or three times. After Cynthia met Jacqueline, she insisted on seeing all of all movies, which was fine with me. But I must admit I also wanted to see them at least once by myself. I can't deny that the affection for Jacqueline was always there, usually buried deep in my subconscious, only to rise to the top whenever she had a new movie.

The last few years were peaceful ones. Jacqueline was always glad to have her special friends come and stay, especially Marcia and Alex, long-time pals not in the entertainment business, but even their visits weren't often anymore as getting to the estate took a bit of planning, and when we hit the November of our years we and our friends were all quite comfortable enjoying our own small slice of the world, with little company or travel.

When Jacqueline got sick it was sudden and devastating. She was gone so fast I was numb and if it hadn't been for her closest friend, Marcia, I would have been a complete basket case. Marcia organized everything until I gained my wits. The only thing I insisted on was that Jacqueline be dressed in the blue blouse.

*

"The Kids"

From the second floor of the 'computer room,' a converted bedroom, I could gaze out at the open land north of our house, tucked in a corner of a small development awaiting completion. Construction had come to a screeching halt three years ago when the housing crisis hit and the remaining homes scheduled to be built were still on the drawing board.

The streets and sidewalks were laid in, the 'Stop' signs were set in place, even at cul de sacs where no automobile traffic had any reason to go, and the street lights and utility boxes sat quietly waiting for people to service.

The look of the empty lots changed with the seasons. Weeds and grasses grew so tall at the intersections you actually had to obey the red and white 'Stop' signs because you couldn't see if there was oncoming traffic. Usually there wouldn't be at the intersection leading to our cul de sac of ten homes. But all it takes is one carless move.

Our few blocks of homes were almost an island, separated from the main residential areas of the city by swaths of empty lots and conservation zones. We had become used to the empty fields, the light traffic—just ourselves—the quiet—except for when one of the kids decided to rev up his motor scooter—and were not looking forward to the continuation of the development. It would bring more traffic, more people, not to mention the noise, dirt, and nails left in the street while the construction was ongoing. I told Caroline we might need to leave for a few months, but I knew that wasn't a practical idea.

In many places, usually close to the sidewalks, bushes had gained a hold and were now taller than the average person. By midsummer the tall grasses had been mowed down and lay like a golden blanket over the ground.

Voles and gophers were happy in their burrowed homes, and jackrabbits frequently flew across the fields. I say flew because their giant hops seemed to cover more territory through the air than they did running across the ground. One would flit across, then another following or chasing it. They would stop, their long ears sticking up like antennae, listening. Then they'd dash off again and cover ground at near-lightning speed, and be gone.

In another empty section, across from where the rabbits had passed, might come a flock of turkeys, moving at a pace totally at odds to that of the rabbits. Head to the ground, picking out seeds and bits of vegetation they'd mosey along, seemingly unconcerned about the encroachment of human habitation. For now, at least. Once construction begins again they will find their pecking grounds reduced.

Farther away, a couple hundred yards north, a creek winds through a conservation belt where trees and other plant life have a solid grip. This area is set aside as a preserve, not to be built on, thank heaven, so we will always have natural areas where we can walk and listen to the songbirds. Signs do warn of dangers: 'Warning: rattlesnake country; stay on paths.' Sound advice.

Some sections of the vacant lots have seen the plant life smashed down by the kids of the neighborhood, who run roughshod chasing each other and playing their games, building forts out of dirt and riding their bikes on the mounds. I will miss seeing them play there, hearing their voices, and looking up from my writing to try to figure out what game they are playing. I was a kid once, too, so I know that the point of kid's games can at times be difficult to discern to an observer.

I will miss the rabbits and the turkeys, too. And most of all I will miss the hawks, if they are pushed out of their hunting territory. These birds of prey are constantly in the sky, floating effortlessly on the currents, watching, and eyeing the land below for movement of an unlucky varmint.

To the south of us the opposite side of the street is lined with houses. But in back of them is another wilderness area where even more wildlife lives and hunts, including coyotes and deer. The turkeys retreat to here each evening and take refuge in the tall trees, where they will bed for the night. Many is the morning I go out front to retrieve the newspaper—yes, I still read a newspaper, despite the Internet—and hear and see the turkeys fly down from their nests and set off in search of the day's sustenance. Their flight, more of a controlled stumble, is not quite as graceful as the hawk's, but it gets the job done.

This area is prime hunting ground for the hawks, but if one decides to expand his territory and moves in the direction of our house, it may fly right over, cutting at an angle towards the open spaces, passing in front of the window through which I view the scene. You can't see them coming; it is sudden and startling but a wonderful reminder of the wild life that still struggles to make a living amongst the creep of civilization.

The sky is not always silent, as when a hawk dives pass the house towards the prey it has sighted, but may be suddenly filled with a roar as a jet fighter from the nearby Air Force base zips by.

Sometimes I can see the F-16s, other times I hear them but can't spot them in the bright blue sky.

At a loss in my story I sit zombie-like staring out the window, watching the kids as they run and chase and ride their bikes up and down the small mounds of dirt that dot the empty lots. Their voices are faint squeals, the exact words not clear at this distance. I slide the window open a few inches and the sounds become louder, but words are still not discernible.

It appears to be a version of 'king of the hill', with the biggest boy, Troy, commanding the hill while several of the younger kids, among them Jessie and Jeff and Billy, Jed and Colt, try to tackle him and pull him down. One of the boys runs back to his bike, which he had dropped at the base of the mound, climbs on and tries to force it uphill, to push the king off his position.

I was fully involved in watching the action now, the story on the computer screen forgotten. From behind the mound a figure was crawling, sneaking up on the king who had fended off the bike rider and was strong enough to take on two or three of the smaller kids at the same time. The screams and cries were of delight; luckily, no serious damage yet to anyone. At least, no blood.

It appeared to be Melanie, a tomboyish girl who was also older than most of the kids, abut the same age as Troy. The king of the hill hadn't seen her yet and I watched with a smile to see if the girl could displace Troy with her sneak attack. Suddenly she reached forward and grabbed Troy by an ankle. He lost his balance and fell. Instantly three or four boys charged and jumped on the bigger boy. They all rolled down the far side of the dirt mound, lost to my view. I could hear screams of triumph.

I turned back to the computer and tried to find my place and regain my focus. What I was working on was a serious drama and I needed to regain the train of thought it required.

For a few minutes I worked diligently, repairing sentences, checking spelling, fixing a word here and there. It was a task I needed to do eventually, and while my mind was not straight on where the story was going next, it gave me something constructive to work on.

After a few minutes I realized I hadn't heard any more noise from outside. I looked towards the mound where I'd last seen the kids playing. They were standing around, no ruckus now, and examining something that Troy held in his hands. From this distance I couldn't see what it was, but it appeared to have the attention of all the kids. The game they'd been playing was over and they were on to something else.

I reached for my binoculars, which I use to spy on the wildlife that passes by my window, and focused on the group of kids. What Troy held in his hand was white and long, like the branch off a birch tree, or a piece of painted wood. He handed it around and each kid took turns with it, waving it in the air as if it were a trophy. Then I noticed one boy, I think it was Jessie, turn and run in the direction of the houses in the cul de sac. His brother and Billy followed him.

A moment later my doorbell rang. I was still trying to ascertain what it was the kids had discovered. Melanie had it now but I couldn't get a good look at it because she kept waving it. I figured I better check the door, probably the UPS guy, when the object came into focus. It looked like the bones of a human arm and hand. The doorbell rang again.

At the door Jeff and Jessie and Billy were waiting and all started to talk as soon as I opened the door.

"You have to come, Mr. Em, hurry!"

"You've got to see this."

"C'mon, c'mon!"

"Let me get my shoes on, boys," I said. I quickly did so and dashed out the door as the boys ran ahead.

"Where you going?" asked Caroline.

"Out with the kids!" I called as I slammed the door.

I don't jog much anymore, having given up such antics once my ankles hurt for three days after each time I dared to do any hard running. I'm good for walks now. But in this case I took off after the boys, trying to keep up with them. I didn't want them to think I was out of shape, oh no.

"Hurry, Mr. Em, you've got to see this!"

Why did they come to me, I asked myself. Then I realized that at this time of day their fathers were either not home, or if they were home, they were working and the boys probably had strict instructions not to bother them until a certain time. But they knew I often saw them playing from my high window.

When I reached the mound Melanie still had the object in her hands. It was as I saw through the binoculars, an arm bone, and it looked genuine. It was definitely bone, not a mockup or a Halloween gadget.

"Where'd you find this, guys?"

"Is it real, Mr. Em?"

"You think somebody got killed here and is buried?"

"We started digging and felt something hard and we just dug it up. Are we gonna be in trouble?"

"Oh, I don't think so, but we'd better call someone," I said. "Let's put it back exactly where you found it."

"It was right here," one of the kids pointed. "Just the tip of it was sticking out, so we started to dig around it."

"You think there's a buried treasure here, too? Like pirate's treasure?"

I had my cell phone with me so I called the local police. They asked if this was a 911 emergency and I said, no, I didn't think so, but that some kids had dug up what looks like human bones, and I thought I should contact the police.

It's not like we had a fresh corpse here, or even an entire skeleton. Still it could be the scene of a crime, albeit an old one. I think we only have nine or ten policemen and women in town, and I guess crime is well under control, because it looked like all of them turned out, plus several members of the fire department, riding high on two trucks, an ambulance, and several plain-clothes cars.

By then I could see a number of people standing at a distance, having heard the traffic noise and seen police and fire vehicles pull up. None of the neighbors came close, and I also noticed that several of my comrades, the kids, had deserted me. Only Melanie and Troy remained. Thanks, guys.

"You the guy who found this body," a uniformed cop asked me.

"It's not a body, just an arm bone. The kids found it."

"What's your name?" he asked.

"Ed Masterson," I replied.

"Masterson? You mean like Bat Masterson, the gunslinger?"

"That was his brother."

"Whose brother?"

"Bat Masterson was Ed Masterson's brother. And he wasn't a gunslinger."

"What are you, a wise guy?" he said, a growl in his voice.

I stared at him, smiled, and said, "What are you, officer, a nincompoop?"

"Wha...? Hey, hey listen here, you want me to take you in for interfering with an investigation?"

I laughed and turned away from him. "Who's in charge here?" I asked to the crowd.

A suit, a detective, I presumed, came over and shunted the uniformed cop aside. "I'll take this, Sergeant. I'm Detective Willis...and you are?"

"Ed Masterson," I said, and waited.

He stuck out his hand and we shook. "You got any brothers?" he asked.

"No, just a sister."

I went on to explain what happened; the kids playing and finding the bone and digging it up.

"And they all got their prints on it, I'll bet," he said.

"Yeah, I suppose. Me too."

"Where are they, the kids? Just these two?" he said, pointing to Troy and Melanie.

"The others are younger. I think they got frightened when they saw police cars coming and they ran home."

Just then I saw Bob and his two boys, Jessie and Jeff, walking over. Bob had come home from work and the boys felt safe in returning to the scene.

"Hey, Ed, what's goin' on?"

Introductions and a brief summary of events were made. By then all the other kids had returned plus several of the adults from the cul de sac walked over. We explained to Detective Willis that we'd all lived here for three years, right from the time the building in this section ceased, and no one remembered or hearing anything that might indicate someone was being buried here.

"In fact, this site was where the construction foreman had his office, one of those portable offices. After they moved it they shoveled dirt around to sort of even the ground, but little by little the kids built mounds as ramps to ride their bikes on."

"We'll have to cordon over this area and treat it as a crime scene for the time being. Make sure the kids don't get in here again." Willis looked at the adults in turn, then at me as if I was the leader.

"Hey, I don't even have any kids," I said, in defense.

"Why'd the kids come to you?"

I shrugged. "They figured I was home and their Dads weren't." I pointed towards my house. "I can see them playing here from my window. They started to toss the ah, bone around, which I didn't know was a bone yet, then some of them ran off. I was looking through my binoculars and I heard the doorbell ring, and so here we are."

"Hmmph," he grunted. "Binoculars, eh? So what else do you see with those spyglasses?"

I resented his insinuation. "They aren't spyglasses, detective. And all I watch are rabbits and kids playing in the dirt."

He grunted again.

The light was dimming and the crowd started to wander off. The authorities would be here for a while longer, securing the site, and we were all warned once again not to come near the area marked by the yellow tape. A few of us decided it was a good evening for pizza. I invited Detective Willis but he declined.

That night, before I retired for the day, I went upstairs and peered out towards the site of today's exciting find. It was too dark to see anything other than a faint wisp of yellow from the police tape. I don't know why I had to look, I just did.

I'm a light sleeper under most conditions so it's not unusual to awaken at two or three in the morning, lie awake and think about things, a story I'm writing, or chores I have to do, or sometimes just listening for the sounds of the night: a lonely train whistle, an even lonelier howl of a coyote, the distant yapping of a dog that someone keeps outdoors so their barking doesn't wake them, only the neighbors, or a mockingbird getting an early start on the day.

When my eyes popped open I saw 2:55 on the clock, and decided to visit the bathroom, as long as I was awake. For a reason I cannot explain I put on my glasses and went upstairs to check on the site of the bone discovery. Again it was too dark to see much; the mound is in the center of an empty lot and the streetlights don't shine that far. Crossing the street at a rapid pace, cutting through the light from the corner lamp, two rabbits caught my eye. Then, out of my peripheral vision, I thought I saw another light, a faint, moving light near the mound.

I strained to see, then picked up my binoculars. There were two shadows moving near the mound. The speck of light I saw probably came from a penlight. Did some of the kids get up in the middle of the night to search for more bones? I couldn't believe it'd be any of the younger kids, but maybe Troy.

If I called the police I'd just get them in trouble. Heck, I remember how much fun it was as a boy to sneak out at night, not necessarily to do anything bad, but just to be out when you weren't supposed to be. But the kids could get in trouble if they messed with the site of the evidence.

I ran downstairs, threw on jeans and shoes, being quiet so I wouldn't wake Caroline, and went out into the night. I had grabbed a flashlight but didn't want to put it on at first, not until I got closer to where the kids were. Maybe I'd scare them a little, just to make them know they got caught at something they shouldn't be doing.

I walked slowly, on tiptoes, as silently as those rabbits that had scurried by. Soon I was close enough to hear voices, whispers and what sounded like digging noises. They must be looking for more bones. The police will be furious. I needed to put an end to this.

"Troy!" I called out, not a shout, but more than a whisper. The noises stopped.

"Troy, is that you? You'd better get away from there. The police are going to be pissed."

The ray from the penlight shot towards me. I turned on my Mag-Lite and pointed back at the beam. It lit on two faces which were instantly covered by hands shielding them from my light. It wasn't Troy; it wasn't anyone I recognized. They were bigger, not kids from the neighborhood.

"Who's there?" I cried. A shudder passed through me and I thought maybe I should high tail it home and call the police. Just as I turned to go I was tackled from a force out of the dark. There was a third person.

I was knocked down and grunted as I hit the dirt and the flashlight fell from my grasp. A hand smacked me in the face, not much of a punch, but enough for me to taste blood on my lips. I pushed back, scared now, and feeling stupid for coming out alone with nothing but a flashlight. I braced myself to be hit again; worse, I feared the sharp rip of a knife; not a gun, obviously these people are trying to be quiet. I didn't have time to think about what they were doing, whether they were souvenir hunters or looking to destroy evidence of some past crime.

There was just enough moonlight to see the face of my attacker. It was a man, not merely an older boy. His face was weathered and mean looking and he sneered at me and punched me in the stomach.

"Oof!" I exhaled.

Desperately I kicked at him but he fell on my chest as if he was trying to smother me. Behind me I heard the sound of the diggers, shoveling hurriedly. Sand was being kicked around by our struggle and I closed my eyes as the grains flew into my face and mouth. My hands and arms flayed wildly in an attempt to knock my attacker away.

"Hurry up you guys," I heard the man say. "I can't keep this guy down forever!"

"Knock him out or somethin'!" one of the diggers called back.

Just as I was feeling frantic and desperately trying to gain enough breath to yell for help, almost panicked now, I heard a clang above me, and the man grappling with me groaned. "Arrgh!"

165

He lost his hold on me and tried to stand up when I heard another clanging sound and the man tumbled over. I rose to my knees, found my flashlight and turned it on. The man was lying on the ground holding his hand over his nose. Blood ran freely down his chin and onto his chest.

Two shadows stood near him and I shone the light on them. It was Bob and Laurie's boys, Jeff and Jessie, the eight and seven-year old brothers who had come to get me earlier, and with whom I'd shared pizza with a few hours ago. They each held a frying pan in their hands.

"Nice going boys! What the heck are you doing out here?"

"Helping you, Mr. Em. We heard noises and came to help you."

"Thanks boys, you did great. Let me have one of those pans."

Jessie gave me his and I stood over the downed man and showed him the pan, daring him to make a move. Tough, aren't I?

The diggers had dropped their shovels and run off into the darkness. I heard a siren and saw the red and blue flashing lights of two patrol cars. One of the cars tore after the fleeing shapes of the former diggers, the other bounced onto the dirt lot and skid to a stop where I stood with Jeff and Jessie, spraying dirt, as if I wasn't dirty enough already. A light shone from behind me. I turned and saw Bob jogging towards our odd group. Caroline and Laurie were following a few yards behind.

"What the hell's going on here, Ed? Jeff, Jessie, what are you doing out here? Are you guys okay, not hurt?"

"We're fine, Dad, sure." Like, of course, what'd you think?

"Did you call the cops, Bob?" I asked.

"Uh? Oh yeah, I heard noises out here and when I looked in their room"—he pointed at his boys—"they weren't there! Laurie was beside herself so she called the cops and I came outside looking for them."

"Well, don't be mad at them, Bob. They conked this one and saved me. I thought I was going to suffocate." I pointed at the conked man who had wrestled with me and been overcome by Jessie and Jeff. Two uniformed police were taking him into custody.

"Yeah, we conked 'em good!" said Jeff.

"Bong, right on the head!" bragged Jessie.

I tousled their hair, each in turn, and smiled at them, a smile that disappeared quickly when Detective Willis walked over.

"So, it's the Wild Bunch again, eh?"

"Hey, Detective Willis," I greeted him. "You want some cold pizza?"

"Hmmph. Sure, as long as the coffee's hot."

We headed for Bob and Laurie's house.

*